Bjørnstjerne Bjørnson

A Happy Boy

and later sketches

Bjørnstjerne Bjørnson

A Happy Boy
and later sketches

ISBN/EAN: 9783337096724

Printed in Europe, USA, Canada, Australia, Japan

Cover: Foto ©Andreas Hilbeck / pixelio.de

More available books at **www.hansebooks.com**

WORKS OF
BJÖRNSTJERNE BJÖRNSON
PATRIOTS EDITION

A HAPPY BOY AND
LATER SKETCHES

Translated from the Norse

By

RASMUS B. ANDERSON

NEW YORK
DOUBLEDAY, PAGE & COMPANY

PREFACE.

———•———

"A HAPPY BOY" was written in 1859 and 1860. It is, in my estimation, Björnson's best story of peasant life. In it the author has succeeded in drawing the characters with *remarkable distinctness*, while his profound psychological insight, his perfectly artless simplicity of style, and his thorough sympathy with the hero and his surroundings are nowhere more apparent. This view is sustained by the great popularity of "A Happy Boy" throughout Scandinavia.

It is proper to add, that in the present edition of Björnson's stories, previous translations have been consulted, and that in this manner a few happy words and phrases have been found and adopted

RASMUS B. ANDERSON.

ASGARD, MADISON, WISCONSIN.
November, 1881

A HASPY BOY.

CHAPTER I.

His name was Öyvind, and he cried when he was born. But no sooner did he sit up on his mother's lap than he laughed, and when the candle was lit in the evening the room rang with his laughter, but he cried when he was not allowed to reach it.

"Something remarkable will come of that boy!" said the mother.

A barren cliff, not a very high one, though, overhung the house where he was born; fir and birch looked down upon the roof, the bird-cherry strewed flowers over it. And on the roof was a little goat belonging to Öyvind; it was kept there that it might not wander away and Öyvind bore leaves and grass up to it. One fine day the goat leaped down and was off to the cliff; it went straight up and soon stood where it had never been before. Öyvind did not see the goat when he came out in the after-

1

noon, and thought at once of the fox. He grew hot all over, and gazing about him, cried, —

" Killy-killy-killy-killy-goat ! "

" Ba-a-a-a ! " answered the goat, from the brow of the hill, putting its head on one side and peering down.

At the side of the goat there was kneeling a little girl.

" Is this goat yours ? " asked she.

Öyvind opened wide his mouth and eyes, thrust both hands into his pants and said, —

" Who are you ? "

" I am Marit, mother's young one, father's fiddle, the hulder of the house, granddaughter to Ola Nordistuen of the Heidegards, four years old in the autumn, two days after the frost nights — I am ! "

" Is that who you are ? " cried he, drawing a long breath, for he had not ventured to take one while she was speaking.

" Is this goat yours ? " she again inquired.

" Ye-es ! " replied he, raising his eyes.

" I have taken such a liking to the goat ; — you will not give it to me ? "

" No, indeed I will not."

She lay kicking up her heels and staring down at him, and presently she said : " But if I give you a twisted bun for the goat, can I have it then ? "

Öyvind was the son of poor people; he had tasted twisted bun only once in his life, that was when grandfather came to his house, and he had never eaten anything equal to it before or since. He fixed his eyes on the girl.

"Let me see the bun first?" said he.

She was not slow in producing a large twisted bun that she held in her hand.

"Here it is!" cried she, and tossed it down to him.

"Oh! it broke in pieces!" exclaimed the boy, picking up every fragment with the utmost care. He could not help tasting of the very smallest morsel, and it was so good that he had to try another piece, and before he knew it himself he had devoured the whole bun.

"Now the goat belongs to me," said the girl.

The boy paused with the last morsel in his mouth; the girl lay there laughing, and the goat stood by her side, with its white breast and shining brown hair, giving sidelong glances down.

"Could you not wait a while," begged the boy, — his heart beginning to throb. Then the girl laughed more than ever, and hurriedly got up on her knees.

"No, the goat is mine," said she, and threw

her arms about it, then loosening one of her
garters she fastened it around its neck. Öyvind watched her. She rose to her feet and began to tug at the goat; it would not go along
with her, and stretched its neck over the edge
of the cliff toward Öyvind.

" Ba-a-a-a !" said the goat.

Then the little girl took hold of its hair with
one hand, pulled at the garter with the other,
and said prettily: " Come, now, goat, you shall
go into the sitting-room and eat from mother's
dish and my apron."

And then she sang, —

> " Come, boy's pretty goatie,
>   Come, calf, my delight,
> Come here, mewing pussie,
>   In shoes snowy white.
> Yellow ducks, from your shelter,
> Come forth, helter-skelter.
> Come, doves, ever beaming,
> With soft feathers gleaming!
>   The grass is still wet,
>   But sun 't will soon get;
> Now call, though early 't is in the summer,
> And autumn will be the new-comer." [1]

There the boy stood.

He had taken care of the goat ever since
winter, when it was born, and it had never occurred to him that he could lose it; but now

---

[1] Auber Forestier's translation.

it was gone in an instant, and he would never see it again.

The mother came trolling up from the beach, with some wooden pails she had been scouring; she saw the boy sitting on the grass, with his legs crossed under him, crying, and went to him.

"What makes you cry?"

"Oh, my goat — my goat!"

"Why, where is the goat?" asked the mother, glancing up at the roof.

"It will never come back any more," said the boy.

"Dear me! how can *that* be?"

Öyvind would not confess at once.

"Has the fox carried it off?"

"Oh, I wish it were the fox!"

"You must have lost your senses!" cried the mother. "What has become of the goat?"

"Oh — oh — oh! I was so unlucky. I sold it for a twisted bun!"

The moment he uttered the words he realized what it was to sell the goat for a bun; he had not thought about it before. The mother said, —

"What do you imagine the little goat thinks of you now, since you were willing to sell it for a twisted bun?"

The boy reflected upon this himself, and felt perfectly sure that he never could know happiness more in *this* world — nor in heaven either, he thought, afterwards.

He was so overwhelmed with sorrow that he promised himself that he would never do anything wrong again, — neither cut the cord of the spinning-wheel, nor let the sheep loose, nor go down to the sea alone. He fell asleep lying there, and he dreamed that the goat had reached heaven. There the Lord was sitting, with a long beard, as in the Catechism, and the goat stood munching at the leaves of a shining tree; but Öyvind sat alone on the roof, and could get no higher. Then something wet was thrust right against his ear, and he started up. " Ba-a-a-a!" he heard, and it was the goat that had returned to him.

"What! have you come back again?" With these words he sprang up, seized it by the two fore-legs, and danced about with it as if it were a brother. He pulled it by the beard, and was on the point of going in to his mother with it, when he heard some one behind him, and saw the little girl sitting on the greensward beside him. Now he understood the whole thing, and he let go of the goat.

" Is it you who have brought the goat?"

She sat tearing up the grass with her hands, and said, "I was not allowed to keep it; grandfather is up there waiting."

While the boy stood staring at her, a sharp voice from the road above called, "Well!"

Then she remembered what she had to do: she rose, walked up to Öyvind, thrust one of her dirt-covered hands into his, and, turning her face away, said, "I beg your pardon."

But then her courage forsook her, and, flinging herself on the goat, she burst into tears.

"I believe you had better keep the goat," faltered Öyvind, looking away.

"Make haste, now!" said her grandfather, from the hill; and Marit got up and walked, with hesitating feet, upward.

"You have forgotten your garter," Öyvind shouted after her. She turned and bestowed a glance, first on the garter, then on him. Finally she formed a great resolve, and replied, in a choked voice, "You may keep it."

He walked up to her, took her by the hand, and said, "I thank you!"

"Oh, there is nothing to thank me for," she answered, and, drawing a piteous sigh, went on.

Öyvind sat down on the grass again, the goat roaming about near him; but he was no longer as happy with it as before.

CHAPTER II.

THE goat was tethered near the house, but Öyvind wandered off, with his eyes fixed on the cliff. The mother came and sat down beside him; he asked her to tell him stories about things that were far away, for now the goat was no longer enough to content him. So his mother told him how once everything could talk: the mountain talked to the brook, and the brook to the river, and the river to the sea, and the sea to the sky; he asked if the sky did not talk to any one, and was told that it talked to the clouds, and the clouds to the trees, the trees to the grass, the grass to the flies, the flies to the beasts, and the beasts to the children, but the children to grown people; and thus it continued until it had gone round in a circle, and neither knew where it had begun. Öyvind gazed at the cliff, the trees, the sea, and the sky, and he had never truly seen them before. The cat came out just then, and stretched itself out on the door-step, in the sunshine.

"What does the cat say?" asked Öyvind and pointed.

The mother sang, —

> "Evening sunshine softly is dying,
> On the door-step lazy puss is lying.
> 'Two small mice,
> Cream so thick and nice;
> Four small bits of fish
> Stole I from a dish;
> Well-filled am I and sleek,
> Am very languid and meek,' —
> Says the pussie." [1]

Then the cock came strutting up with all the hens.

"What does the cock say?" asked Öyvind, clapping his hands.

The mother sang, —

> "Mother-hen her wings now are sinking,
> Chanticleer on one leg stands thinking:
> 'High, indeed,
> Yon wild goose can speed;
> Never, surely though, she
> Clever as a cock can be.
> Seek your shelter, hens, I pray,
> Gone is the sun to his rest for to-day,' —
> Says the rooster." [1]

Two small birds sat singing on the gable.

"What are the birds saying?" asked Öyvind, and laughed.

> "'Dear Lord, how pleasant is life,
> For those who have neither toil nor strife,' —
> Say the birds." [2]

— was the answer.

[1] Auber Forestier's translation.
[2] Translated by H. R. G.

Thus he learned what all were saying, even
to the ant crawling in the moss and the worm
working in the bark.

The same summer his mother undertook to
teach him to read. He had had books for a
long time, and wondered how it would be when
they, too, should begin to talk. Now the letters
were transformed into beasts and birds and all
living creatures; and soon they began to move
about together, two and two; *a* stood resting
beneath a tree called *b*, *c* came and joined it;
but when three or four were grouped together
they seemed to get angry with one another, and
nothing would then go right. The farther he
advanced the more completely he found himself
forgetting what the letters were; he longest remembered *a*, which he liked best; it was a little
black lamb and was on friendly terms with all
the rest; but soon *a*, too, was forgotten, the
books no longer contained stories, only lessons.

Then one day his mother came in and said to
him, —

"To-morrow school begins again, and you
are going with me up to the gard."

Öyvind had heard that school was a place
where many boys played together, and he had
nothing against that. He was greatly pleased ·
he had often been to the gard, but not when

there was school there, and he walked faster than his mother up the hill-side, so eager was he. When they came to the house of the old people, who lived on their annuity, a loud buzzing, like that from the mill at home, met them, and he asked his mother what it was.

"It is the children reading," answered she, and he was delighted, for thus it was that he had read before he learned the letters.

On entering he saw so many children round a table that there could not be more at church; others sat on their dinner-pails along the wall, some stood in little knots about an arithmetic table; the school-master, an old, gray-haired man, sat on a stool by the hearth, filling his pipe. They all looked up when Öyvind and his mother came in, and the clatter ceased as if the mill-stream had been turned off. Every eye was fixed on the new-comers; the mother saluted the school-master, who returned her greeting.

"I have come here to bring a little boy who wants to learn to read," said the mother.

"What is the fellow's name?" inquired the school-master, fumbling down in his leathern pouch after tobacco.

"Öyvind," replied the mother, "he knows his letters and he can spell."

" You do not say so ! " exclaimed the school-master. " Come here, you white-head ! "

" Öyvind walked up to him, the school-master took him up on his knee and removed his cap.

" What a nice little boy ! " said he, stroking the child's hair. Öyvind looked up into his eyes and laughed.

" Are you laughing at me ! " The old man knit his brow, as he spoke.

" Yes, I am," replied Öyvind, with a merry peal of laughter.

Then the school-master laughed, too; the mother laughed; the children knew now that they had permission to laugh, and so they all laughed together.

With this Öyvind was initiated into school.

When he was to take his seat, all the scholars wished to make room for him ; he on his part looked about for a long time ; while the other children whispered and pointed, he turned in every direction, his cap in his hand, his book under his arm.

" Well, what now ? " asked the school-master, who was again busied with his pipe.

Just as the boy was about turning toward the school-master, he espied, near the hearth-stone close beside him, sitting on a little red painted box, Marit with the many names; she had hidden her face behind both hands and sat peeping out at him.

"I will sit here!" cried Öyvind, promptly, and seizing a lunch-box he seated himself at her side. Now she raised the arm nearest him a little and peered at him from under her elbow; forthwith he, too, covered his face with both hands and looked at her from under his elbow. Thus they sat cutting up capers until she laughed, and then he laughed also; the other little folks noticed this, and they joined in the laughter; suddenly a voice which was frightfully strong, but which grew milder as it spoke, interposed with, —

"Silence, troll-children, wretches, chatter-boxes! — hush, and be good to me, sugar-pigs!"

It was the school-master, who had a habit of flaring up, but becoming good-natured again before he was through. Immediately there was quiet in the school, until the pepper grinders again began to go; they read aloud, each from his book; the most delicate trebles piped up, the rougher voices drumming louder and louder in order to gain the ascendency, and here and there one chimed in, louder than the others. In all his life Öyvind had never had such fun.

" Is it always so here ? " he whispered to Marit.

" Yes, always," said she.

Later they had to go forward to the school-master and read ; a little boy was afterwards appointed to teach them to read, and then they were allowed to go and sit quietly down again.

" I have a goat now myself," said Marit.

" Have you ? "

" Yes, but it is not as pretty as yours."

" Why do you never come up to the cliff again ? "

" Grandfather is afraid I might fall over."

" Why, it is not so very high."

" Grandfather will not let me, nevertheless."

" Mother knows a great many songs," said Öyvind.

" Grandfather does, too, I can tell you.

" Yes, but he does not know mother's songs."

" Grandfather knows one about a dance. Do you want to hear it ? "

" Yes, very much."

" Well, then, come nearer this way, that the school-master may not see us."

He moved close to her, and then she recited a little snatch of a song, four or five times, until the boy learned it, and it was the first thing he learned at school.

"Dance!" cried the fiddle;
  Its strings all were quaking,
  The lensmand's son making
  Spring up and say "Ho!"
"Stay!" called out Ola,
  And tripped him up lightly;
  The girls laughed out brightly,
  The lensmand lay low.

"Hop!" said then Erik,
  His heel upward flinging;
  The beams fell to ringing,
  The walls gave a shriek.
"Stop!" shouted Elling,
  His collar then grasping,
  And held him up, gasping:
  "Why, you're far too weak!"

"Hey!" spoke up Rasmus,
  Fair Randi then seizing;
"Come, give without teasing
  That kiss. Oh! you know!"
"Nay!" answered Randi,
  And boxing him smartly,
  Dashed off, crying tartly:
"Take that now and go!" [1]

"Up, youngsters!" cried the school-master, "this is the first day, so you shall be let off early; but first we must say a prayer and sing."

The whole school was now alive; the little folks jumped down from the benches, ran across the floor and all spoke at once.

"Silence, little gypsies, young rascals, yearlings!—be still and walk nicely across the floor,

[1] Auber Forestier's translation.

little children ! " said the school-master, and
they quietly took their places, after which the
school-master stood in front of them and made
a short prayer. Then they sang ; the school-
master started the tune, in a deep bass ; all the
children, folding their hands, joined in. Öyvind
stood at the foot, near the door, with Marit,
looking on ; they also clasped their hands, but
they could not sing.

This was the first day at school.

CHAPTER III.

ÖYVIND grew and became a clever boy; he was among the first scholars at school, and at home he was faithful in all his tasks. This was because at home he loved his mother and at school the school-master; he saw but little of his father, who was always either off fishing or was attending to the mill, where half the parish had their grinding done.

What had the most influence on his mind in these days was the school-master's history, which his mother related to him one evening as they sat by the hearth. It sank into his books, it thrust itself beneath every word the school-master spoke, it lurked in the school-room when all was still. It caused him to be obedient and reverent, and to have an easier apprehension as it were of everything that was taught him.

The history ran thus : —

The school-master's name was Baard, and he once had a brother whose name was Anders. They thought a great deal of each other; they both enlisted; they lived together in the town,

and took part in the war, both being made cor-
porals, and serving in the same company. On
their return home after the war, every one
thought they were two splendid fellows. Now
their father died; he had a good deal of per-
sonal property, which was not easy to divide,
but the brothers decided, in order that this
should be no cause of disagreement between
them, to put the things up at auction, so that
each might buy what he wanted, and the pro-
ceeds could be divided between them. No
sooner said than done. Their father had owned
a large gold watch, which had a wide-spread
fame, because it was the only gold watch people in that part of the country had seen, and
when it was put up many a rich man tried to
get it until the two brothers began to take part
in the bidding; then the rest ceased. Now,
Baard expected Anders to let him have the
watch, and Anders expected the same of
Baard; each bid in his turn to put the other
to the test, and they looked hard at each other
while bidding. When the watch had been run
up to twenty dollars, it seemed to Baard that
his brother was not acting rightly, and he continued to bid until he got it almost up to
thirty; as Anders kept on, it struck Baard that
his brother could not remember how kind he

had always been to him, nor that he was the elder of the two, and the watch went up to over thirty dollars. Anders still kept on. Then Baard suddenly bid forty dollars, and ceased to look at his brother. It grew very still in the auction-room, the voice of the lens-mand alone was heard calmly naming the price. Anders, standing there, thought if Baard could afford to give forty dollars he could also, and if Baard grudged him the watch, he might as well take it. He bid higher. This Baard felt to be the greatest disgrace that had ever befallen him; he bid fifty dollars, in a very low tone. Many people stood around, and Anders did not see how his brother could so mock at him in the hearing of all; he bid higher. At length Baard laughed.

"A hundred dollars and my brotherly affection in the bargain," said he, and turning left the room. A little later, some one came out to him, just as he was engaged in saddling the horse he had bought a short time before.

"The watch is yours," said the man; "Anders has withdrawn."

The moment Baard heard this there passed through him a feeling of compunction; he thought of his brother, and not of the watch. The horse was saddled, but Baard paused with his hand on its back, uncertain whether to ride away or no. Now many people came out, among them Anders, who when he saw his brother standing beside the saddled horse, not knowing what Baard was reflecting on, shouted out to him : —

" Thank you for the watch, Baard! You will not see it run the day your brother treads on your heels."

" Nor the day I ride to the gard again," replied Baard, his face very white, swinging himself into the saddle.

Neither of them ever again set foot in the house where they had lived with their father.

A short time after, Anders married into a houseman's family; but Baard was not invited to the wedding, nor was he even at church. The first year of Anders' marriage the only cow he owned was found dead beyond the north side of the house, where it was tethered, and no one could find out what had killed it. Several misfortunes followed, and he kept going down-hill; but the worst of all was when his barn, with all that it contained, burned down in the middle of the winter ; no one knew how the fire had originated.

" This has been done by some one who wishes me ill," said Anders, — and he wept that night. He was now a poor man and had lost all ambition for work.

The next evening Baard appeared in his room. Anders was in bed when he entered, but sprang directly up.

"What do you want here?" he cried, then stood silent, staring fixedly at his brother.

Baard waited a little before he answered, —

"I wish to offer you help, Anders; things are going badly for you."

"I am faring as you meant I should, Baard! Go, I am not sure that I can control myself."

"You mistake, Anders; I repent" —

"Go, Baard, or God be merciful to us both!"

Baard fell back a few steps, and with quivering voice he murmured, —

"If you want the watch you shall have it."

"Go, Baard!" shrieked the other, and Baard left, not daring to linger longer.

Now with Baard it had been as follows: As soon as he had heard of his brother's misfortunes, his heart melted; but pride held him back. He felt impelled to go to church, and there he made good resolves, but he was not able to carry them out. Often he got far enough to see Anders' house; but now some one came out of the door; now there was a

stranger there; again Anders was outside chop-
ping wood, so there was always something in
the way. But one Sunday, late in the winter,
he went to church again, and Anders was there
too. Baard saw him; he had grown pale and
thin; he wore the same clothes as in former
days when the brothers were constant companions, but now they were old and patched. During the sermon Anders kept his eyes fixed on
the priest, and Baard thought he looked good
and kind; he remembered their childhood and
what a good boy Anders had been. Baard
went to communion that day, and he made a
solemn vow to his God that he would be recon-
ciled with his brother whatever might happen.
This determination passed through his soul
while he was drinking the wine, and when he
rose he wanted to go right to him and sit down
beside him; but some one was in the way and
Anders did not look up. After service, too,
there was something in the way; there were
too many people; Anders' wife was walking at
his side, and Baard was not acquainted with
her; he concluded that it would be best to go
to his brother's house and have a serious talk
with him. When evening came he set forth.
He went straight to the sitting-room door and
listened, then he heard his name spoken; it was
by the wife.

" He took the sacrament to-day," said she ;
' he surely thought of you."

" No ; he did not think of me," said Anders.
" I know him ; he thinks only of himself."

For a long time there was silence ; the sweat
poured from Baard as he stood there, although
it was a cold evening. The wife inside was
busied with a kettle that crackled and hissed
on the hearth ; a little infant cried now and
then, and Anders rocked it. At last the wife
spoke these few words : —

" I believe you both think of each other without being willing to admit it."

" Let us talk of something else," replied
Anders."

After a while he got up and moved towards
the door. Baard was forced to hide in the
wood-shed ; but to that very place Anders came
to get an armful of wood. Baard stood in the
corner and saw him distinctly ; he had put off
his threadbare Sunday clothes and wore the
uniform he had brought home with him from
the war, the match to Baard's, and which he
had promised his brother never to touch but to
leave for an heirloom, Baard having given him
a similar promise. Anders' uniform was now
patched and worn ; his strong, well-built frame
was encased, as it were, in a bundle of rags

and, at the same time, Baard heard the gold watch ticking in his own pocket. Anders walked to where the fagots lay; instead of stooping at once to pick them up, he paused, leaned back against the wood-pile and gazed up at the sky, which glittered brightly with stars. Then he drew a sigh and muttered, —

" Yes — yes — yes; — O Lord ! O Lord !"

As long as Baard lived he heard these words. He wanted to step forward, but just then his brother coughed, and it seemed so difficult, more was not required to hold him back. Anders took up his armful of wood, and brushed past Baard, coming so close to him that the twigs struck his face, making it smart.

For fully ten minutes he stood as if riveted to the spot, and it is doubtful when he would have left, had he not, after his great emotion, been seized with a shivering fit that shook him through and through. Then he moved away; he frankly confessed to himself that he was too cowardly to go in, and so he now formed a new plan. From an ash-box which stood in the corner he had just left, he took some bits of charcoal, found a resinous pine-splint, went up to the barn, closed the door and struck a light. When he had lit the pine-splint, he held it up to find the wooden peg where Anders hung his lantern

when he came early in the morning to thresh.
Baard took his gold watch and hung it on the
peg, blew out his light and left; and then he
felt so relieved that he bounded over the snow
like a young boy.

The next day he heard that the barn had
burned to the ground during the night. No
doubt sparks had fallen from the torch that
had lit him while he was hanging up his
watch.

This so overwhelmed him that he kept his
room all day like a sick man, brought out his
hymn-book, and sang until the people in the
house thought he had gone mad. But in the
evening he went out; it was bright moonlight.
He walked to his brother's place, dug in the
ground where the fire had been, and found, as
he had expected, a little melted lump of gold.
It was the watch.

It was with this in his tightly closed hand
that he went in to his brother, imploring peace,
and was about to explain everything.

A little girl had seen him digging in the
ashes, some boys on their way to a dance had
noticed him going down toward the place the
preceding Sunday evening; the people in the
house where he lived testified how curiously he
had acted on Monday and as every one knew

that he and his brother were bitter enemies, information was given and a suit instituted.

No one could prove anything against Baard, but suspicion rested on him. Less than ever, now, did he feel able to approach his brother.

Anders had thought of Baard when the barn was burned, but had spoken of it to no one. When he saw him enter his room, the following evening, pale and excited, he immediately thought: "Now he is smitten with remorse, but for such a terrible crime against his brother he shall have no forgiveness." Afterwards he heard how people had seen Baard go down to the barn the evening of the fire, and, although nothing was brought to light at the trial, Anders firmly believed his brother to be guilty.

They met at the trial; Baard in his good clothes, Anders in his patched ones. Baard looked at his brother as he entered, and his eyes wore so piteous an expression of entreaty that Anders felt it in the inmost depths of his heart. "He does not want me to say anything," thought Anders, and when he was asked if he suspected his brother of the deed, he said loudly and decidedly, "No!"

Anders took to hard drinking from that day, and was soon far on the road to ruin. Still worse was it with Baard; although he did not drink, he was scarcely to be recognized by those who had known him before.

Late one evening a poor woman entered the little room Baard rented, and begged him to accompany her a short distance. He knew her: it was his brother's wife. Baard understood forthwith what her errand was; he grew deathly pale, dressed himself, and went with her without a word. There was a glimmer of light from Anders' window, it twinkled and disappeared, and they were guided by this light, for there was no path across the snow. When Baard stood once more in the passage, a strange odor met him which made him feel ill. They entered. A little child stood by the fireplace eating charcoal; its whole face was black, but as it looked up and laughed it displayed white teeth, — it was the brother's child.

There on the bed, with a heap of clothes thrown over him, lay Anders, emaciated, with smooth, high forehead, and with his hollow eyes fixed on his brother. Baard's knees trembled; he sat down at the foot of the bed and burst into a violent fit of weeping. The sick man looked at him intently and said nothing. At length he asked his wife to go out, but Baard made a sign to her to remain; and now these two brothers began to talk together.

3

They accounted for everything from the day they had bid for the watch up to the present moment. Baard concluded by producing the lump of gold he always carried about him, and it now became manifest to the brothers that in all these years neither had known a happy day.

Anders did not say much, for he was not able to do so, but Baard watched by his bed as long as he was ill.

"Now I am perfectly well," said Anders one morning on waking. "Now, my brother, we will live long together, and never leave each other, just as in the old days."

But that day he died.

Baard took charge of the wife and the child, and they fared well from that time. What the brothers had talked of together by the bed, burst through the walls and the night, and was soon known to all the people in the parish, and Baard became the most respected man among them. He was honored as one who had known great sorrow and found happiness again, or as one who had been absent for a very long time. Baard grew inwardly strong through all this friendliness about him; he became a truly pious man, and wanted to be useful, he said, and so the old corporal took to teaching school. What he impressed upon the children, first and last, was love, and he practiced it himself, so that the children clung to him as to a playmate and father in one.

Such was the history of the school-master, and so deeply did it root itself in Öyvind's mind that it became both religion and education for him. The school-master grew to be almost a supernatural being in his eyes, although he sat there so sociably, grumbling at the scholars. Not to know every lesson for him was impossible, and if Öyvind got a smile or a pat on his head after he had recited, he felt warm and happy for a whole day.

It always made the deepest impression on the children when the old school-master sometimes before singing made a little speech to them, and at least once a week read aloud some verses about loving one's neighbor. When he read the first of those verses, his voice always trembled, although he had been reading it now some twenty or thirty years. It ran thus:—

> "Love thy neighbor with Christian zeal!
> Crush him not with an iron heel,
>   Though he in dust be prostrated!
> Love's all powerful, quickening hand
> Guides, forever, with magic wand
>   All that it has created."

But when he had recited the whole poem

and had paused a little, he would cry, and his eyes would twinkle, —

" Up, small trolls! and go nicely home without any noise, — go quietly, that I may only hear good of you, little toddlers! "

But when they were making the most noise in hunting up their books and dinner-pails, he shouted above it all, —

" Come again to morrow, as soon as it is light, or I will give you a thrashing. Come again in good season, little girls and boys, and then we will be industrious."

CHAPTER IV.

Of Öyvind's further progress until a year before confirmation there is not much to report. He studied in the morning, worked through the day, and played in the evening.

As he had an unusually sprightly disposition, it was not long before the neighboring children fell into the habit of resorting in their playtime to where he was to be found. A large hill sloped down to the bay in front of the place, bordered by the cliff on one side and the wood on the other, as before described; and all winter long, on pleasant evenings and on Sundays, this served as coasting-ground for the parish young folks. Öyvind was master of the hill, and he owned two sleds, "Fleet-foot" and "Idler;" the latter he loaned out to larger parties, the former he managed himself, holding Marit on his lap.

The first thing Öyvind did in those days on awaking, was to look out and see whether it was thawing, and if it was gray and lowering over the bushes beyond the bay, or if he heard

309134

a dripping from the roof, he was long about dressing, as though there were nothing to be accomplished that day.   But if he awoke, especially on a Sunday, to crisp, frosty, clear weather, to his best clothes and no work, only catechism or church in the morning, with the whole afternoon and evening free — heigh ! then the boy made one spring out of bed, donned his clothes in a hurry as if for a fire, and could scarcely eat a mouthful.   As soon as afternoon had come, and the first boy on skees drew in sight along the road-side, swinging his guide-pole above his head and shouting so that echoes resounded through the mountain-ridges about the lake ; and then another on the road on a sled, and still another and another, — off started Öyvind with " Fleet-foot," bounded down the hill, and stopped among the last-comers, with a long, ringing shout that pealed from ridge to ridge all along the bay, and died away in the far distance.

Then he would look round ıor Marit, but when she had come he payed no further attention to her.

At last there came a Christmas, whı ' Öyvind and Marit might be about sixteen or seventeen and were both to be confirmed in the spring. The fourth day after Christmas there was a party at the upper Heidegards, at Marit's grandparents', by whom she had been brought up, and who had been promising her this party for three years, and now at last had to give it during the holidays. Öyvind was invited to it.

It was a somewhat cloudy evening but not cold; no stars could be seen; the next day must surely bring rain. There blew a sleepy wind over the snow, which was swept away here and there on the white Heidefields; elsewhere it had drifted. Along the part of the road where there was but little snow, were smooth sheets of ice of a blue-black hue, lying between the snow and the bare field, and glittering in patches as far as the eye could reach. Along the mountain-sides there had been avalanches; it was dark and bare in their track, but on either side light and snow-clad, except where the forest birch-trees put their heads together and made dark shadows. No water was visible, but half-naked heaths and bogs lay under the deeply-fissured, melancholy mountains. Gards were spread in thick clusters in the centre of the plain; in the gloom of the winter evening they resembled black clumps, from which light shot out over the fields, now from one window, now from another; from these lights it might be judged that those within were busy.

Young people, grown-up and half-grown-up, were flocking together from diverse directions; only a few of them came by the road, the others had left it at least when they approached the gards, and stole onward, one behind the stable, a couple near the store-house, some stayed for a long time behind the barn, screaming like foxes, others answered from afar like cats; one stood behind the smoke-house, barking like a cross old dog whose upper notes were cracked; and at last all joined in a general chase. The girls came sauntering along in large groups, having a few boys, mostly small ones, with them, who had gathered about them on the road in order to appear like young men. When such a bevy of girls arrived at the gard and one or two of the grown youths saw them, the girls parted, flew into the passages or down in the garden, and had to be dragged thence into the house, one by one. Some were so excessively bashful that Marit had to be sent for, and then she came out and insisted upon their entering. Sometimes, too, there appeared one who had had no invitation and who had by no means intended to go in, coming only to look on, until perhaps she might have a chance just to take one single dance. Those whom Marit liked well she invited into a small chamber where her grandfather sat smoking his pipe, and her grandmother was walking about. The old people offered them something to drink and spoke kindly to them. Öyvind was not among those invited in, and this seemed to him rather strange.

The best fiddler of the parish could not come until later, so meanwhile they had to content themselves with the old one, a houseman, who went by the name of Gray-Knut. He knew four dances; as follows: two spring dances, a halling, and an old dance, called the Napoleon waltz; but gradually he had been compelled to transform the halling into a schottishe by altering the accent, and in the same manner a spring dance had to become a polka-mazurka. He now struck up and the dancing began. Öyvind did not dare join in at once, for there were too many grown folks here; but the half-grown-up ones soon united, thrust one another forward, drank a little strong ale to strengthen their courage, and then Öyvind came forward with them. The room grew warm to them; merriment and ale mounted to their heads. Marit was on the floor most of the time that evening, no doubt because the party was at her grandparents'; and this led Öyvind to look frequently at her; but she was always dancing

with others. He longed to dance with her himself, and so he sat through one dance, in order
to be able to hasten to her side the moment it
was ended; and he did so, but a tall, swarthy
fellow, with thick hair, threw himself in his
way.

"Back, youngster!" he shouted, and gave
Öyvind a push that nearly made him fall back-
wards over Marit.

Never before had such a thing occurred to
Öyvind; never had any one been otherwise than
kind to him; never had he been called "youngster" when he wanted to take part; he blushed
crimson, but said nothing, and drew back to
the place where the new fiddler, who had just
arrived, had taken his seat and was tuning his
instrument. There was silence in the crowd,
every one was waiting to hear the first vigorous
tones from "the chief fiddler." He tried his
instrument and kept on tuning; this lasted a
long time; but finally he began with a spring
dance, the boys shouted and leaped, couple after
couple coming into the circle. Öyvind watched
Marit dancing with the thick-haired man; she
laughed over the man's shoulder and her white
teeth glistened. Öyvind felt a strange, sharp
pain in his heart for the first time in his life.

He looked longer and longer at her, but how

ever it might be, it seemed to him that Marit
was now a young maiden. "It cannot be so,
though," thought he, "for she still takes part
with the rest of us in our coasting." But
grown-up she was, nevertheless, and after the
dance was ended, the dark-haired man pulled
her down on his lap; she tore herself away,
but still she sat down beside him.

Öyvind's eyes turned to the man, who wore
a fine blue broadcloth suit, blue checked shirt,
and a soft silk neckerchief; he had a small face,
vigorous blue eyes, a laughing, defiant mouth.
He was handsome. Öyvind looked more and
more intently, finally scanned himself also; he
had had new trousers for Christmas, which he
had taken much delight in, but now he saw
that they were only gray wadmal; his jacket
was of the same material, but old and dark; his
vest, of checked homespun, was also old, and
had two bright buttons and a black one. He
glanced around him and it seemed to him that
very few were so poorly clad as he. Marit wore
a black, close-fitting dress of a fine material, a
silver brooch in her neckerchief and had a
folded silk handkerchief in her hand. On the
back of her head was perched a little black
silk cap, which was tied under the chin with a
broad, striped silk ribbon. She was fair and

had rosy cheeks, and she was laughing; the man was talking to her and was laughing too. The fiddler started another tune, and the dancing was about to begin again. A comrade came and sat down beside Öyvind.

"Why are you not dancing, Öyvind?" he asked pleasantly.

"Dear me!" said Öyvind, "I do not look fit."

"Do not look fit?" cried his comrade; but before he could say more, Öyvind inquired, —

"Who is that in the blue broadcloth suit, dancing with Marit?"

"That is Jon Hatlen, he who has been away so long at an agricultural school and is now to take the gard."

At that moment Marit and Jon sat down.

"Who is that boy with light hair sitting yonder by the fiddler, staring at me?" asked Jon.

Then Marit laughed and said, —

"He is the son of the houseman at Pladsen."

Öyvind had always known that he was a houseman's son; but until now he had never realized it. It made him feel so very little, smaller than all the rest; in order to keep up he had to try and think of all that hitherto had made him happy and proud, from the coasting hill to each kind word. He thought, too, of his mother and his father, who were now sitting at home and thinking that he was having a good time, and he could scarcely hold back his tears. Around him all were laughing and joking, the fiddle rang right into his ear, it was a moment in which something black seemed to rise up before him, but then he remembered the school with all his companions, and the school-master who patted him, and the priest who at the last examination had given him a book and told him he was a clever boy. His father himself had sat by listening and had smiled on him.

"Be good now, dear Öyvind," he thought he heard the school-master say, taking him on his lap, as when he was a child. "Dear me! it all matters so little, and in fact all people are kind; it merely seems as if they were not. We two will be clever, Öyvind, just as clever as Jon Hatlen; we shall yet have good clothes, and dance with Marit in a light room, with a hundred people in it; we will smile and talk together; there will be a bride and bridegroom, a priest, and I will be in the choir smiling upon you, and mother will be at home, and there will be a large gard with twenty cows, three horses, and Marit as good and kind as at school."

The dancing ceased. Öyvind saw Marit on the bench in front of him, and Jon by her side with his face close up to hers; again there came that great burning pain in his breast, and he seemed to be saying to himself: "It is true, I am suffering."

Just then Marit rose, and she came straight to him. She stooped over him.

"You must not sit there staring so fixedly at me," said she; "you might know that people are noticing it. Take some one now and join the dancers."

He made no reply, but he could not keep back the tears that welled up to his eyes as he looked at her. Marit had already risen to go when she saw this, and paused; suddenly she grew as red as fire, turned and went back to her place, but having arrived there she turned again and took another seat. Jon followed her forthwith.

Öyvind got up from the bench, passed through the crowd, out in the grounds, sat down on a porch, and then, not knowing what he wanted there rose, but sat down again, thinking he might just as well sit there as any-where else. He did not care about going home, nor did he desire to go in again, it was all one to him. He was not capable of considering

what had happened ; he did not want to think
of it ; neither did he wish to think of the future, for there was nothing to which he looked
forward.

" But what, then, is it I am thinking of?" he
queried, half aloud, and when he had heard his
own voice, he thought: "You can still speak,
can you laugh?" And then he tried it ; yes,
he could laugh, and so he laughed loud, still
louder, and then it occurred to him that it was
very amusing to be sitting laughing here all
by himself, and he laughed again. But Hans,
the comrade who had been sitting beside him,
came out after him.

" Good gracious, what are you laughing at?"
he asked, pausing in front of the porch. At
this Öyvind was silent.

Hans remained standing, as if waiting to see
what further might happen. Öyvind got up,
looked cautiously about him and said in a low
tone, —

"Now Hans, I will tell you why I have been
so happy before: it was because I did not really
love any one ; from the day we love some one,
we cease to be happy," and he burst into tears.

"Öyvind!" a voice whispered out in the
court ; " Öyvind!" He paused and listened.
" Öyvind," was repeated once more, a little
louder. " It must be she," he thought.

"Yes," he answered, also in a whisper; and hastily wiping his eyes he came forward.

A woman stole softly across the gard.

"Are you there?" she asked.

"Yes," he answered, standing still.

"Who is with you?"

"Hans."

But Hans wanted to go.

"No, no!" besought Öyvind.

She slowly drew near them, and it was Marit.

"You left so soon," said she to Öyvind.

He knew not what to reply; thereupon Marit, too, became embarrassed, and all three were silent. But Hans gradually managed to steal away. The two remained behind, neither looking at each other, nor stirring. Finally Marit whispered: —

"I have been keeping some Christmas goodies in my pocket for you, Öyvind, the whole evening, but I have had no chance to give them to you before."

She drew forth some apples, a slice of a cake from town, and a little half pint bottle, which she thrust into his hand, and said he might keep. Öyvind took them.

"Thank you!" said he, holding out his hand; hers was warm, and he dropped it at once as if it had burned him.

" You have danced a good deal this evening,"
he murmured.

" Yes, I have," she replied, " but *you* have
not danced much," she added.

" I have not," he rejoined.

" Why did you not dance ? "

" Oh " —

" Öyvind ! "

" Yes."

" Why did you sit looking at me so ? "

" Oh — Marit ! "

" What ! "

" Why did you dislike having me look at
you ? "

" There were so many people."

" You danced a great deal with Jon Hatlen
this evening."

" I did."

" He dances well."

" Do you think so ? "

" Oh, yes. I do not know how it is, but this
evening I could not bear to have you dance
with him, Marit."

He turned away, — it had cost him something
to say this.

" I do not understand you, Öyvind."

" Nor do I understand myself; it is very stupid of me. Good-by, Marit; I will go now."

4

He made a step forward without looking round. Then she called after him.

"You make a mistake about what you saw."

He stopped.

"That you have already become a maiden is no mistake."

He did not say what she had expected, therefore she was silent; but at that moment she saw the light from a pipe right in front of her. It was her grandfather, who had just turned the corner and was coming that way. He stood still.

"Is it here you are, Marit?"

"Yes."

"With whom are you talking?"

"With Öyvind."

"Whom did you say?"

"Öyvind Pladsen."

"Oh! the son of the houseman at Pladsen. Come at once and go in with me."

CHAPTER V.

THE next morning, when Öyvind opened his eyes, it was from a long, refreshing sleep and happy dreams. Marit had been lying on the cliff, throwing leaves down on him; he had caught them and tossed them back again, so they had gone up and down in a thousand colors and forms; the sun was shining, and the whole cliff glittered beneath its rays. On awaking Öyvind looked around to find them all gone; then he remembered the day before, and the burning, cruel pain in his heart began at once. "This, I shall never be rid of again," thought he; and there came over him a feeling of indifference, as though his whole future had dropped away from him.

"Why, you have slept a long time," said his mother, who sat beside him spinning. "Get up now and eat your breakfast; your father is already in the forest cutting wood."

Her voice seemed to help him; he rose with a little more courage. His mother was no doubt thinking of her own dancing days, for

she sat singing to the sound of the spinning-
wheel, while he dressed himself and ate his
breakfast. Her humming finally made him
rise from the table and go to the window; the
same dullness and depression he had felt before
took possession of him now, and he was forced
to rouse himself, and think of work. The
weather had changed, there had come a little
frost into the air, so that what yesterday had
threatened to fall in rain, to-day came down as
sleet. Öyvind put on his snow-socks, a fur
cap, his sailor's jacket and mittens, said farewell, and started off, with his axe on his
shoulder.

Snow fell slowly, in great, wet flakes; he
toiled up over the coasting hill, in order to turn
into the forest on the left. Never before, winter or summer, had he climbed this hill without recalling something that made him happy,
or to which he was looking forward. Now it
was a dull, weary walk. He slipped in the
damp snow, his knees were stiff, either from
the party yesterday or from his low spirits; he
felt that it was all over with the coasting-hill
for that year, and with it, forever. He longed
for something different as he threaded his way
in among the tree-trunks, where the snow fell
softly. A frightened ptarmigan screamed and

fluttered a few yards away, but everything else stood as if awaiting a word which never was spoken. But what his aspirations were, he did not distinctly know, only they concerned nothing at home, nothing abroad, neither pleasure nor work ; but rather something far above, soaring upward like a song. Soon all became concentrated in one defined desire, and this was to be confirmed in the spring, and on that occasion to be number one. His heart beat wildly as he thought of it, and before he could yet hear his father's axe in the quivering little trees, this wish throbbed within him with more intensity than anything he had known in all his life.

His father, as usual, did not have much to say to him ; they chopped away together and both dragged the wood into heaps. Now and then they chanced to meet, and on one such occasion Öyvind remarked, in a melancholy tone, " A houseman has to work very hard."

" He as well as others," said the father, as he spit in the palm of his hand and took up the axe again.

When the tree was felled and the father had drawn it up to the pile, Öyvind said, —

" If you were a gardman you would not have to work so hard."

" Oh ! then there would doubtless be other

things to distress us," and he grasped his axe with both hands.

The mother came up with dinner for them; they sat down. The mother was in high spirits, she sat humming and beating time with her feet.

"What are you going to make of yourself when you are grown up, Öyvind?" said she, suddenly.

"For a houseman's son, there are not many openings," he replied.

"The school-master says you must go to the seminary," said she.

"Can people go there free?" inquired Öyvind.

"The school-fund pays," answered the father, who was eating.

"Would you like to go?" asked the mother.

"I should like to learn something, but not to become a school-master."

They were all silent for a time. The mother hummed again and gazed before her; but Öyvind went off and sat down by himself.

"We do not actually need to borrow of the school-fund," said the mother, when the boy was gone.

Her husband looked at her.

"Such poor folks as we?"

" It does not please me, Thore, to have you always passing yourself off for poor when you are not so."

They both stole glances down after the boy to find out if he could hear. The father looked sharply at his wife.

" You talk as though you were very wise."

She laughed.

" It is just the same as not thanking God that things have prospered with us," said she, growing serious.

" We can surely thank Him without wearing silver buttons," observed the father.

" Yes, but to let Öyvind go to the dance, dressed as he was yesterday, is not thanking Him either."

" Öyvind is a houseman's son."

" That is no reason why he should not wear suitable clothes when we can afford it."

" Talk about it so he can hear it himself!"

" He does not hear it; but I should like to have him do so," said she, and looked bravely at her husband, who was gloomy, and laid down his spoon to take his pipe.

" Such a poor houseman's place as we have!" said he.

" I have to laugh at you, always talking about the place, as you are. Why do you never speak of the mills ? "

" Oh! you and the mills. I believe you cannot bear to hear them go."

" Yes, I can, thank God! might they but go
night and day ! "

" They have stood still now, since before
Christmas."

"Folks do not grind here about Christmas
time."

" They grind when there is water; but since
there has been a mill at New Stream, we have
fared badly here."

" The school-master did not say so to-day."

"I shall get a more discreet fellow than the
school-master to manage our money."

" Yes, he ought least of all to talk with your
own wife."

Thore made no reply to this; he had just lit
his pipe, and now, leaning up against a bundle
of fagots, he let his eyes wander, first from his
wife, then from his son, and fixed them on an
old crow's-nest which hung, half overturned,
from a fir-branch above.

Öyvind sat by himself with the future stretch-
ing before him like a long, smooth sheet of ice,
across which for the first time he found himself
sweeping onward from shore to shore. That
poverty hemmed him in on every side, he felt,
but for that reason his whole mind was bent on

breaking through it. From Marit it had un-
doubtedly parted him forever; he regarded her
as half engaged to Jon Hatlen; but he had determined to vie with him and her through the
entire race of life. Never again to be rebuffed
as he had been yesterday, and in view of this to
keep out of the way until he made something
of himself, and then, with the aid of Almighty
God, to continue to be something, — occupied
all his thoughts, and there arose within his soul
not a single doubt of his success. He had a dim
idea that through study he would get on best;
to what goal it would lead he must consider
later.

There was coasting in the evening; the children came to the hill, but Öyvind was not with
them. He sat reading by the fire-place, feeling
that he had not a moment to lose. The children waited a long time; at length, one and
another became impatient, approached the
house, and laying their faces against the window-pane shouted in; but Öyvind pretended
not to hear them. Others came, and evening
after evening they lingered about outside, in
great surprise; but Öyvind turned his back to
them and went on reading, striving faithfully
to gather the meaning of the words. Afterwards he heard that Marit was not there either.

He read with a diligence which even his father was forced to say went too far. He became grave; his face, which had been so round and soft, grew thinner and sharper, his eye more stern; he rarely sang, and never played; the right time never seemed to come. When the temptation to do so beset him, he felt as if some one whispered, "later, later!" and always "later!" The children slid, shouted, and laughed a while as of old, but when they failed to entice him out either through his own love of coasting, or by shouting to him with their faces pressed against the window-pane, they gradually fell away, found other playgrounds, and soon the hill was deserted.

But the school-master soon noticed that this was not the old Öyvind who read because it was his turn, and played because it was a necessity. He often talked with him, coaxed and admonished him; but he did not succeed in finding his way to the boy's heart so easily as in days of old. He spoke also with the parents, the result of the conference being that he came down one Sunday evening, late in the winter, and said, after he had sat a while, —

"Come now, Öyvind, let us go out; I want to have a talk with you."

Öyvind put on his things and went with him.

They wended their way up toward the Heidegards; a brisk conversation was kept up, but
about nothing in particular; when they drew
near the gards the school-master turned aside
in the direction of one that lay in the centre,
and when they had advanced a little farther,
shouting and merriment met them.

"What is going on here?" asked Öyvind.

"There is a dance here," said the school-
master; "shall we not go in?"

"No."

"Will you not take part in a dance, boy?"

"No; not yet."

"Not yet? When, then?"

Öyvind did not answer.

"What do you mean by *yet?*"   .

As the youth did not answer, the school-master said, —

"Come, now, no such nonsense."

"No, I will not go."

He was very decided and at the same time
agitated.

"The idea of your own school-master standing here and begging you to go to a dance."

There was a long pause.

"Is there any one in there whom you are
afraid to see?"

"I am sure I cannot tell who may be in
there."

" But is there likely to be any one ? "

Öyvind was silent. Then the school-master walked straight up to him, and laying his hand on his shoulder, said, —

" Are you afraid to see Marit ? "

Öyvind looked down ; his breathing became heavy and quick.

" Tell me, Öyvind, my boy ? "

Öyvind made no reply.

" You are perhaps ashamed to confess it since you are not yet confirmed ; but tell me, nevertheless, my dear Öyvind, and you shall not regret it."

Öyvind raised his eyes but could not speak the word, and let his gaze wander away.

" You are not happy, either, of late. Does she care more for any one else than for you ? "

Öyvind was still silent, and the school-master, feeling slightly hurt, turned away from him. They retraced their steps.

After they had walked a long distance, the school-master paused long enough for Öyvind to come up to his side.

" I presume you are very anxious to be confirmed," said he.

" Yes."

" What do you think of doing afterwards ? '

" I should like to go to the seminary."

"And then become a school-master?"

"No."

"You do not think that is great enough?"

Öyvind made no reply. Again they walked on for some distance.

"When you have been through the seminary, what will you do?"

"I have not fairly considered that."

"If you had money, I dare say you would like to buy yourself a gard?"

"Yes, but keep the mills."

"Then you had better enter the agricultural school."

"Do pupils learn as much there as at the seminary?"

"Oh, no! but they learn what they can make use of later."

"Do they get numbers there too?"

"Why do you ask?"

"I should like to be a good scholar."

"That you can surely be without a number."

They walked on in silence again until they saw Pladsen; a light shone from the house, the cliff hanging over it was black now in the winter evening; the lake below was covered with smooth, glittering ice, but there was no snow on the forest skirting the silent bay; the moon

sailed overhead, mirroring the forest trees in
the ice.

"It is beautiful here at Pladsen," said the
school-master.

There were times when Öyvind could see
these things with the same eyes with which
he looked when his mother told him nursery
tales, or with the vision he had when he coasted
on the hill-side, and this was one of those times,
— all lay exalted and purified before him.

"Yes, it is beautiful," said he, but he sighed.

"Your father has found everything he
wanted in this home; you, too, might be con
tented here."

The joyous aspect of the spot suddenly disappeared. The school-master stood as if awaiting an answer; receiving none, he shook his
head and entered the house with Öyvind. He
sat a while with the family, but was rather
silent than talkative, whereupon the others too
became silent. When he took his leave, both
husband and wife followed him outside of the
door; it seemed as if both expected him to say
something. Meanwhile, they stood gazing up
into the night.

"It has grown so unusually quiet here,"
finally said the mother, "since the children
have gone away with their sports."

" Nor have you a *child* in the house any longer, either," said the school-master.

The mother knew what he meant.

"Öyvind has not been happy of late," said
she.

" Ah, no! he who is ambitious never is
happy," — and he gazed up with an old man's
calmness into God's peaceful heavens above.

CHAPTER VI.

HALF a year later — in the autumn it was (the confirmation had been postponed until then) — the candidates for confirmation of the main parish sat in the parsonage servant's hall, waiting examination, among them were Öyvind Pladsen and Marit Heidegards. Marit had just come down from the priest, from whom she had received a handsome book and much praise; she laughed and chatted with her girl friends on all sides and glanced around among the boys. Marit was a full-grown girl, easy and frank in her whole address, and the boys as well as the girls knew that Jon Hatlen, the best match in the parish, was courting her, — well might she be happy as she sat there. Down by the door stood some girls and boys who had not passed; they were crying, while Marit and her friends were laughing; among them was a little boy in his father's boots and his mother's Sunday kerchief.

"Oh, dear! oh, dear!" sobbed he, "I dare not go home again."

And this overcame those who had not yet been up with the power of sympathy; there was a universal silence. Anxiety filled their throats and eyes; they could not see distinctly, neither could they swallow; and this they felt a continual desire to do.

One sat reckoning over how much he knew; and although but a few hours before he had discovered that he knew everything, now he found out just as confidently that he knew nothing, not even how to read in a book.

Another summed up the list of his sins, from the time he was large enough to remember until now, and he decided that it would not be at all remarkable if the Lord decreed that he should be rejected.

A third sat taking note of all things about him: if the clock which was about to strike did not make its first stroke before he could count twenty, he would pass; if the person he heard in the passage proved to be the gard-boy Lars, he would pass; if the great rain-drop, working its way down over the pane, came as far as the moulding of the window, he would pass. The final and decisive proof was to be if he succeeded in twisting his right foot about the left, — and this it was quite impossible for him to do.

A fourth was convinced in his own mind that if he was only questioned about Joseph in Bible history and about baptism in the Catechism, or about Saul, or about domestic duties, or about Jesus, or about the Commandments, or — he still sat rehearsing when he was called.

A fifth had taken a special fancy to the Sermon on the Mount; he had dreamed about the Sermon on the Mount; he was sure of being questioned on the Sermon on the Mount; he kept repeating the Sermon on the Mount to himself; he had to go out doors and read over the Sermon on the Mount — when he was called up to be examined on the great and the small prophets.

A sixth thought of the priest who was an excellent man and knew his father so well; he thought, too, of the school-master, who had such a kindly face, and of God who was all goodness and mercy, and who had aided so many before both Jacob and Joseph; and then he remembered that his mother and brothers and sisters were at home praying for him, which surely must help.

The seventh renounced all he had meant to become in this world. Once he had thought that he would like to push on as far as being a king, once as far as general or priest; now

that time was over. But even to the moment
of his coming here he had thought of going to
sea and becoming a captain, perhaps a pirate,
and acquiring enormous riches; now he gave
up first the riches, then the pirate, then the
captain, then the mate; he paused at sailor, at
the utmost boatswain; indeed, it was possible
that he would not go to sea at all, but would
take a houseman's place on his father's gard.

The eighth was more hopeful about his case
but not certain, for even the aptest scholar was
not certain. He thought of the clothes he was
to be confirmed in, wondering what they would
be used for if he did not pass. But if he passed
he was going to town to get a broadcloth suit,
and coming home again to dance at Christmas
to the envy of all the boys and the astonishment of all the girls.

The ninth reckoned otherwise: he prepared a
little account book with the Lord, in which he
set down on one side, as it were, " Debit: " he
must let me pass, and on the other "Credit: "
then I will never tell any more lies, never tittle-
tattle any more, always go to church, let the
girls alone, and break myself of swearing.

The tenth, however, thought that if Ole
Hansen had passed last year it would be more
than unjust if he who had always done better

at school, and, moreover, came of a better family, did not get through this year.

By his side sat the eleventh, who was wrestling with the most alarming plans of revenge in the event of his not being passed: either to burn down the school-house, or to run away from the parish and come back again as the denouncing judge of the priest and the whole school commission, but magnanimously allow mercy to take the place of justice. To begin with, he would take service at the house of the priest of the neighboring parish, and there stand number one next year, and answer so that the whole church would marvel.

But the twelfth sat alone under the clock, with both hands in his pockets, and looked mournfully out over the assemblage. No one here knew what a burden he bore, what a responsibility he had assumed. At home there was one who knew, — for he was betrothed. A large, long-legged spider was crawling over the floor and drew near his foot; he was in the habit of treading on this loathsome insect, but to-day he tenderly raised his foot that it might go in peace whither it would. His voice was as gentle as a collect, his eyes said incessantly that all men were good, his hands made a humble movement out of his pockets up to his hair to stroke it down more smoothly. If he could only glide gently through this dangerous needle's eye, he would doubtless grow out again on the other side, chew tobacco, and announce his engagement.

And down on a low stool with his legs drawn up under him, sat the anxious thirteenth; his little flashing eyes sped round the room three times each second, and through the passionate, obstinate head stormed in motley confusion the combined thoughts of the other twelve: from the mightiest hope to the most crushing doubt, from the most humble resolves to the most devastating plans of revenge; and, meanwhile, he had eaten up all the loose flesh on his right thumb, and was busied now with his nails, sending large pieces across the floor.

Öyvind sat by the window, he had been upstairs and had answered everything that had been asked him; but the priest had not said anything, neither had the school-master. For more than half a year he had been considering what they both would say when they came to know how hard he had toiled, and he felt now deeply disappointed as well as wounded. There sat Marit, who for far less exertion and knowledge had received both encouragement and reward; it was just in order to stand high in her

eyes that he had striven, and now she smilingly
won what he had labored with so much self-
denial to attain. Her laughter and joking
burned into his soul, the freedom with which
she moved about pained him. He had carefully
avoided speaking with her since that evening,
it would take years, he thought; but the sight
of her sitting there so happy and superior,
weighed him to the ground, and all his proud
determinations drooped like leaves after a rain.

He strove gradually to shake off his depression. Everything depended on whether he became number one to-day, and for this he was
waiting. It was the school-master's wont to
linger a little after the rest with the priest to
arrange about the order of the young people,
and afterwards to go down and report the result; it was, to be sure, not the final decision,
merely what the priest and he had for the
present agreed upon. The conversation became livelier after a considerable number had
been examined and passed; but now the ambitious ones plainly distinguished themselves
from the happy ones; the latter left as soon
as they found company, in order to announce
their good fortune to their parents, or they
waited for the sake of others who were not
yet ready; the former, on the contrary, grew

more and more silent and their eyes were fixed
in suspense on the door.

At length the children were all through, the
last had come down, and so the school-master
must now be talking with the priest. Öyvind
glanced at Marit; she was just as happy as before, but she remained in her seat, whether
waiting for her own pleasure or for some one
else, he knew not. How pretty Marit had become! He had never seen so dazzlingly lovely
a complexion; her nose was slightly turned up,
and a dainty smile played about the mouth.
She kept her eyes partially closed when not
looking directly at any one, but for that reason
her gaze always had unsuspected power when
it did come; and, as though she wished herself
to add that she meant nothing by this, she half
smiled at the same moment. Her hair was
rather dark than light, but it was wavy and
crept far over the brow on either side, so that,
together with the half closed eyes, it gave the
face a hidden expression that one could never
weary of studying. It never seemed quite sure
whom it was she was looking for when she was
sitting alone and among others, nor what she
really had in mind when she turned to speak to
any one, for she took back immediately, as it
were, what she gave. " Under all this Jon

Hatlen is hidden, I suppose," thought Öyvind but still stared constantly at her.

Now came the school-master. All left their places and stormed about him.

" What number am I ? " — " And I ? " — " And I — I ? "

" Hush! you overgrown young ones! No uproar here! Be quiet and you shall hear about it, children." He looked slowly around. " You are number two," said he to a boy with blue eyes, who was gazing up at him most beseechingly; and the boy danced out of the circle. " You are number three," he tapped a redhaired, active little fellow who stood tugging at his jacket. " You are number five; you number eight," and so on. Here he caught sight of Marit. " You are number one of the girls," — she blushed crimson over face and neck, but tried to smile. " You are number twelve; you have been lazy, you rogue, and full of mischief; you number eleven, nothing better to be expected, my boy; you, number thirteen, must study hard and come to the next examination, or it will go badly with you ! "

Öyvind could bear it no longer; number one, to be sure, had not been mentioned, but he had been standing all the time so that the school-master could see him.

"School - master!" He did not hear. "School-master!" Öyvind had to repeat this three times before it was heard. At last the school-master looked at him.

"Number nine or ten, I do not remember which," said he, and turned to another.

"Who is number one, then?" inquired Hans, who was Öyvind's best friend.

"It is not you, curly-head!" said the school-master, rapping him over the hand with a roll of paper.

"Who is it, then?" asked others. "Who is t? Yes; who is it?"

"He will find that out who has the number," replied the school-master, sternly. "He would have no more questions. Now go home nicely, children. Give thanks to your God and gladden your parents. Thank your old school-master too; you would have been in a pretty fix if it had not been for him."

They thanked him, laughed, and went their way jubilantly, for at this moment when they were about to go home to their parents they all felt happy. Only one remained behind, who could not at once find his books, and who when he had found them sat down as if he must read them over again.

The school-master went up to him.

" Well, Öyvind, are you not going with the rest? "

There was no reply.

" Why do you open your books? "

"I want to find out what I answered wrong to-day."

" You answered nothing wrong."

Then Öyvind looked up with tears in his eyes ; but he continued to gaze intently at the school-master, while the tears one by one trickled down his cheeks, and not a word did he say. The school-master sat down in front of him.

" Are you not glad that you passed ? "

There was a quivering about the lips but no reply.

" Your mother and father will be very glad," said the school-master, and looked at Öyvind.

The boy struggled hard to gain power of utterance, finally he asked in low, broken tones, —

" Is it — because I — am a houseman's son that I only stand number nine or ten ? "

"No doubt that was it," replied the school-master.

" Then it is of no use for me to work," said Öyvind, drearily, and all his bright dreams vanished. Suddenly he raised his head, lifted his right hand, and bringing it down on the table with all his might, flung himself forward on his face and burst into passionate tears.

The school-master let him lie and weep, — weep as long as he would. It lasted a long time, but the school-master waited until the weeping grew more childlike. Then taking Öyvind's head in both hands, he raised it and gazed into the tear-stained face.

" Do you believe that it is God who has been with you now," said he, drawing the boy affectionately toward him.

Öyvind was still sobbing, but not so violently as before ; his tears flowed more calmly, but he neither dared look at him who questioned nor answer.

" This, Öyvind, has been a well-merited recompense. You have not studied from love of your religion, or of your parents ; you have studied from vanity."

There was silence in the room after every sentence the school-master uttered. Öyvind felt his gaze resting on him, and he melted and grew humble under it.

" With such wrath in your heart, you could not have come forward to make a covenant with your God. Do you think you could, Öy vind ? "

" No," the boy stammered, as well as he was able.

"And if you stood there with vain joy, over being number one, would you not be coming forward with a sin?"

"Yes, I should," whispered Öyvind, and his lips quivered.

"You still love me, Öyvind?"

"Yes;" here he looked up for the first time.

"Then I will tell you that it was I who had you put down; for I am very fond of you, Öyvind."

The other looked at him, blinked several times, and the tears rolled down in rapid succession.

"You are not displeased with me for that?"

"No;" he looked up full in the school-master's face, although his voice was choked.

"My dear child, I will stand by you as long as I live."

The school-master waited for Öyvind until the latter had gathered together his books, then said that he would accompany him home. They walked slowly along. At first Öyvind was silent and his struggle went on, but gradually he gained his self-control. He was convinced that what had occurred was the best thing that in any way could have happened to him; and before he reached home, his belief in this had become so strong that he gave thanks to his God, and told the school-master so.

"Yes, now we can think of accomplishing something in life," said the school-master, "instead of playing blind-man's buff, and chasing after numbers. What do you say to the seminary?"

"Why, I should like very much to go there."

"Are you thinking of the agricultural school?"

"Yes."

"That is, without doubt, the best; it provides other openings than a school-master's position."

"But how can I go there? I earnestly desire it, but I have not the means."

"Be industrious and good, and I dare say the means will be found."

Öyvind felt completely overwhelmed with gratitude. His eyes sparkled, his breath came lightly, he glowed with that infinite love that bears us along when we experience some unexpected kindness from a fellow-creature. At such a moment, we fancy that our whole future will be like wandering in the fresh mountain air; we are wafted along more than we walk.

When they reached home both parents were within, and had been sitting there in quiet expectation, although it was during working hours of a busy time. The school-master en-

tered first, Oyvind followed; both were smiling.

" Well?" said the father, laying aside a
hymn-book, in which he had just been reading
a " Prayer for a Confirmation Candidate."

His mother stood by the hearth, not daring
to say anything; she was smiling, but her hand
was trembling. Evidently she was expecting
good news, but did not wish to betray herself.

" I merely had to come to gladden you with
the news, that he answered every question put
. to him ; and that the priest said, when Oyvind
had left him, that he had never had a more apt
scholar."

" Is it possible ! " said the mother, much affected.

" Well, that is good," said his father, clear-
ing his throat unsteadily.

After it had been still for some time, the
mother asked, softly, —

" What number will he have?"

" Number nine or ten," said the school-master, calmly.

The mother looked at the father ; he first at
her, then at Öyvind, and said, —

" A houseman's son can expect no more."

Öyvind returned his gaze. Something rose
up in his throat once more, but he hastily

forced himself to think of things that he loved, one by one, until it was choked down again.

" Now I had better go," said the school-master, and nodding, turned away.

Both parents followed him as usual out on the door-step; here the school-master took a quid of tobacco, and smiling said, —

" He will be number one, after all ; but it is not worth while that he should know anything about it until the day comes."

" No, no," said the father, and nodded.

" No, no," said the mother, and she nodded too ; after which she grasped the school-master's hand and added : " We thank you for all you do for him."

" Yes, you have our thanks," said the father, and the school-master moved away.

They long stood there gazing after him.

CHAPTER VII.

THE school-master had judged the boy correctly when he asked the priest to try whether Öyvind could bear to stand number one. During the three weeks which elapsed before the confirmation, he was with the boy every day. It is one thing for a young, tender soul to yield to an impression; what through faith it shall attain is another thing. Many dark hours fell upon Öyvind before he learned to choose the goal of his future from something better than ambition and defiance. Often in the midst of his work he lost his interest and stopped short: what was it all for, what would he gain by it? — and then presently he would remember the school-master, his words and his kindness; and this human medium forced him to rise up again every time he fell from a comprehension of his higher duty.

In those days while they were preparing at Pladsen for the confirmation, they were also preparing for Öyvind's departure for the agricultural school, for this was to take place the

following day. Tailor and shoemaker were
sitting in the family-room; the mother was bak-
ing in the kitchen, the father working at a
chest. There was a great deal said about what
Öyvind would cost his parents in the next two
years; about his not being able to come home
the first Christmas, perhaps not the second
either, and how hard it would be to be parted
so long. They spoke also of the love Öyvind
should bear his parents who were willing to
sacrifice themselves for their child's sake. Öyvind sat like one who had tried sailing out into
the world on his own responsibility, but had
been wrecked and was now picked up by kind
people.

Such is the feeling that humility gives, and
with it comes much more. As the great day
drew near he dared call himself prepared, and
also dared look forward with trustful resigna-
tion. Whenever Marit's image would present
itself, he cautiously thrust it aside, although he
felt a pang in so doing. He tried to gain practice in this, but never made any progress in
strength; on the contrary, it was the pain that
grew. Therefore he was weary the last evening, when, after a long self-examination, he
prayed that the Lord would not put him to the
test in this matter

The school-master came as the day was draw-ing to a close. They all sat down together in the family-room, after washing and dressing themselves neat and clean, as was customary the evening before going to communion, or morning service. The mother was agitated, the father silent; parting was to follow the morrow's ceremony, and it was uncertain when they could all sit down together again. The school-master brought out the hymn-books, read the service, sang with the family, and after-wards said a short prayer, just as the words came into his mind.

These four people now sat together until late in the evening, the thoughts of each centering within; then they parted with the best wishes for the coming day and what it was to conse-crate. Öyvind was obliged to admit, as he laid himself down, that he had never gone to bed so happy before; he gave this an interpre-tation of his own, — he understood it to mean: I have never before gone to bed feeling so resigned to God's will and so happy in it. Marit's face at once rose up before him again, and the last thing he was conscious of was that he lay and examined himself: not quite happy, not quite, — and that he answered: yes, quite, but again: not quite; yes, quite; no, not quite

When he awoke he at once remembered the day, prayed, and felt strong, as one does in the morning. Since the summer, he had slept alone in the attic; now he rose, and put on his handsome new clothes, very carefully, for he had never owned such before. There was especially a round broadcloth jacket, which he had to examine over and over again before he became accustomed to it. He hung up a little looking-glass when he had adjusted his collar, and for the fourth time drew on his jacket. At sight of his own contented face, with the unusually light hair surrounding it, reflected and smiling in the glass, it occurred to him that this must certainly be vanity again. "Yes, but people must be well-dressed and tidy," he reasoned, drawing his face away from the glass, as if it were a sin to look in it. "To be sure, but not quite so delighted with themselves, for the sake of the matter." "No, certainly not, but the Lord must also like to have one care to look well." "That may be; but He would surely like it better to have you do so without making so much notice of it yourself." "That is true; but it happens now because everything is so new." "Yes, but you must gradually lay the habit aside." — He caught himself carrying on such a self-examining conversation.

now upon one theme, now upon another, so that not a sin should fall on the day and stain it; but at the same time he knew that he had other struggles to meet.

When he came down-stairs, his parents sat all dressed, waiting breakfast for him. He went up to them and taking their hands thanked them for the clothes, and received in return a "wear-them-out-with-good-health." [1] They sat down to table, prayed silently, and ate. The mother cleared the table, and carried in the lunch-box for the journey to church. The father put on his jacket, the mother fastened her kerchief; they took their hymn-books, locked up the house, and started. As soon as they had reached the upper road they met the church-faring people, driving and walking, the confirmation candidates scattered among them, and in one group and another white-haired grand-parents, who had felt moved to come out on this great occasion.

It was an autumn day without sunshine, as when the weather is about to change. Clouds gathered together and dispersed again; some-times out of one great mass were formed twenty smaller ones, which sped across the sky with

[1] A common expression among the peasantry of Norway, meaning: "You are welcome."

orders for a storm ; but below, on the earth, it
was still calm, the foliage hung lifeless, not a
leaf stirring; the air was a trifle sultry ; people
carried their outer wraps with them but did not
use them. An unusually large multitude had
assembled round the church, which stood in an
open space; but the confirmation children immediately went into the church in order to be
arranged in their places before service began.
Then it was that the school-master, in a blue
broadcloth suit, frock coat, and knee-breeches,
high shoes, stiff cravat, and a pipe protruding
from his back coat pocket, came down towards
them, nodded and smiled, tapped one on the
shoulder, spoke a few words to another about
answering loudly and distinctly, and meanwhile
worked his way along to the poor-box, where
Öyvind stood answering all the questions of his
friend Hans in reference to his journey.

" Good-day, Öyvind. How fine you look to-
day ! " He took him by the jacket collar as
if he wished to speak to him. " Listen. I
believe everything good of you. I have been
talking with the priest; you will be allowed to
keep your place ; go up to number one and answer distinctly ! "

Öyvind looked up at him amazed ; the school-
master nodded ; the boy took a few steps,

stopped, a few steps more, stopped again : " Yes,
it surely is so; he has spoken to the priest for
me," — and the boy walked swiftly up to his
place.

" You are to be number one, after all," some
one whispered to him.

" Yes," answered Öyvind, in a low voice, but
did not feel quite sure yet whether he dared
think so.

The assignment of places was over, the priest
had come, the bells were ringing, and the people pouring into church.   Then Öyvind saw
Marit Heidegards just in front of him ; she saw
him too; but they were both so awed by the
sacredness of the place that they dared not
greet each other.   He only noticed that she
was dazzlingly beautiful and that her hair was
uncovered ; more he did not see.   Öyvind, who
for more than half a year had been building
such great plans about standing opposite her,
forgot, now that it had come to the point, both
the place and her, and that he had in any way
thought of them.

After all was ended the relatives and acquaintances came up to offer their congratula-
tions ; next came Öyvind's comrades to take
leave of him, as they had heard that he was to
depart the next day; then there came many

little ones with whom he had coasted on the hill-sides and whom he had assisted at school, and who now could not help whimpering a little at parting. Last came the school-master, silently took Öyvind and his parents by the hands, and made a sign to start for home; he wanted to accompany them. The four were together once more, and this was to be the last evening. On the way home they met many others who took leave of Öyvind and wished him good luck; but they had no other conversation until they sat down together in the family-room.

The school-master tried to keep them in good spirits; the fact was now that the time had come they all shrank from the two long years of separation, for up to this time they had never been parted a single day; but none of them would acknowledge it. The later it grew the more dejected Öyvind became; he was forced to go out to recover his composure a little.

It was dusk now and there were strange sounds in the air. Öyvind remained standing on the door-step gazing upward. From the brow of the cliff he then heard his own name called, quite softly; it was no delusion, for it was repeated twice. He looked up and faintly distinguished a female form crouching between the trees and looking down.

"Who is it?" asked he.

"I hear you are going away," said a low voice, "so I had to come to you and say good-by, as you would not come to me."

"Dear me! Is that you, Marit? I shall come up to you."

"No, pray do not. I have waited so long, and if you come I should have to wait still longer; no one knows where I am and I must hurry home."

"It was kind of you to come," said he.

"I could not bear to have you leave so, Öyvind; we have known each other since we were children."

"Yes; we have."

"And now we have not spoken to each other for half a year."

"No; we have not."

"We parted so strangely, too, that time."

"We did. I think I must come up to you!"

"Oh, no! do not come! But tell me: you are not angry with me?"

"Goodness! how could you think so?"

"Good-by, then, Öyvind, and my thanks for all the happy times we have had together!"

" Wait, Marit ! "

" Indeed I must go ; they will miss me."

" Marit ! Marit ! "

" No, I dare not stay away any longer, Öy-vind. Good-by."

" Good-by ! "

Afterwards he moved about as in a dream, and answered very absently when he was addressed. This was ascribed to his journey, as was quite natural ; and indeed it occupied his whole mind at the moment when the schoolmaster took leave of him in the evening and put something into his hand, which he afterwards found to be a five-dollar bill. But later, when he went to bed, he thought not of the journey, but of the words which had come down from the brow of the cliff, and those that had been sent up again. As a child Marit was not allowed to come on the cliff, because her grandfather feared she might fall down. Perhaps she will come down some day, any way.

CHAPTER VIII.

DEAR PARENTS, — We have to study much more now than at first, but as I am less behind the others than I was, it is not so hard. I shall change many things in father's place when I come home; for there is much that is wrong there, and it is wonderful that it has prospered as well as it has. But I shall make everything right, for I have learned a great deal. I want to go to some place where I can put into practice all I now know, and so I must look for a high position when I get through here.

No one here considers Jon Hatlen as clever as he is thought to be at home with us; but as he has a gard of his own, this does not concern any one but himself.

Many who go from here get very high salaries, but they are paid so well because ours is the best agricultural school in the country. Some say the one in the next district is better, but this is by no means true. There are two words here: one is called Theory, the other Practice. It is well to have them both, for one is nothing without the other; but still the latter is the better. Now the former means, to understand the cause and principle of a work; the latter, to be able to perform it: as, for instance, in regard to a quagmire; for there are many who know what should be done with a quagmire and yet do it wrong, because they are not able to put their knowledge into practice. Many, on the other hand, are skillful in doing, but do not know what ought to be done; and thus they too may make bad work of it, for there are many kinds of quagmires. But we at the agricultural school learn both words. The superintendent is so skillful that he has no equal. At the last agricultural meeting for the whole country, he led in two discussions, and the other superintendents had only one each, and upon careful consideration his statements were always sustained. At the meeting before the last, where he was not present, there was nothing but idle talk. The lieutenant who teaches surveying was chosen by the superintendent only on account of his ability, for the other schools have no lieutenant. He is so clever that he was the best scholar at the military academy.

The school-master asks if I go to church. Yes, of course I go to church, for now the priest has an assistant, and his sermons fill all the congregation with terror, and it is a pleasure to listen to him. He belongs to the new religion they have in Christiania, and people think him too strict, but it is good for them that he is so.

Just now we are studying much history, which we have not done before, and it is curious to observe all that has happened in the world, but especially in our country, for we have always won, except when we have lost, and then we always had the smaller number. We now have liberty; and no other nation has so much of it as we, except America; but there they are not happy. Our freedom should be loved by us above everything.

Now I will close for this time, for I have written a very long letter. The school-master will read it, I suppose, and when he answers for you, get him to tell me some news about one thing or another, for he never does so of himself. But now accept hearty greetings from your affectionate son,

Ö. THORESEN.

DEAR PARENTS,—Now I must tell you that we have had examinations, and that I stood excellent' in many things, and 'very good in writing and surveying, but 'good' in Norwegian composition. This comes, the superin-

tendent says, from my not having read enough,
and he has made me a present of some of Ole
Vig's books, which are matchless, for I understand everything in them. The superintendent is very kind to me, and he tells us many
things. Everything here is very inferior compared with what they have abroad; we understand almost nothing, but learn everything
from the Scotch and Swiss, although horticult-
ure we learn from the Dutch. Many visit
these countries. In Sweden, too, they are
much more clever than we, and there the superintendent himself has been. I have been
here now nearly a year, and I thought that I
had learned a great deal; but when I heard
what those who passed the examination knew,
and considered that they would not amount to
anything either when they came into contact
with foreigners, I became very despondent.
And then the soil here in Norway is so poor
compared with what it is abroad; it does not
at all repay us for what we do with it. Moreover, people will not learn from the experience
of others; and even if they would, and if the
soil was much better, they really have not the
money to cultivate it. It is remarkable that
things have prospered as well as they have.

I am now in the highest class, and am to re-

main there a year before I get through. But
most of my companions have left and I long for
home. I feel alone, although I am not so by
any means, but one has such a strange feeling
when one has been long absent. I once thought
I should become so much of a scholar here; but
I am not making the progress I anticipated.

What shall I do with myself when I leave
here? First, of course, I will come home;
afterwards, I suppose, I will have to seek something to do, but it must not be far away.

Farewell, now, dear parents! Give greetings
to all who inquire for me, and tell them that I
have everything pleasant here but that now I
long to be at home again.

Your affectionate son,
ÖYVIND THORESEN PLADSEN.

DEAR SCHOOL-MASTER, — With this I ask
if you will deliver the inclosed letter and not
speak of it to any one. And if you will not,
then you must burn it.

ÖYVIND THORESEN PLADSEN.

To THE MOST HONORED MAIDEN, MARIT KNUDSDAT-
TER NORDISTUEN AT THE UPPER HEIDEGARDS: —

You will no doubt be much surprised at receiving a letter from me; but you need not

be for I only wish to ask how you are. You must send me a few words as soon as possible, giving me all particulars. Regarding myself, I have to say that I shall be through here in a year. Most respectfully,

ÖYVIND PLADSEN.

TO ÖYVIND PLADSEN, AT THE AGRICULTURAL SCHOOL : —

Your letter was duly received by me from the school-master, and I will answer since you request it. But I am afraid to do so, now that you are so learned; and I have a letter-writer, but it does not help me. So I will have to try what I can do, and you must take the will for the deed; but do not show this, for if you do you are not the one I think you are. Nor must you keep it, for then some one might see it, but you must burn it, and this you will have to promise me to do. There were so many things I wanted to write about, but I do not quite dare. We have had a good harvest; potatoes bring a high price, and here at the Heidegards we have plenty of them. But the bear has done much mischief among the cattle this summer: he killed two of Ole Nedregard's cattle and injured one belonging to our houseman so badly that it had to be killed for beef. I am weaving a large piece of cloth, something like a Scotch plaid, and it is difficult. And now I will tell you that I am still at home, and that there are those who would like to have it otherwise. Now I have no more to write about for this time, and so I must bid you farewell.

MARIT KNUDSDATTER.

P. S. — Be sure and burn this letter.

To THE AGRICULTURIST, ÖYVIND THORESEN PLADSEN : —

As I have told you before, Öyvind, he who walks with God has come into the good inheritance. But now you must listen to my advice, and that is not to take the world with yearning and tribulation, but to trust in God and not allow your heart to consume you, for if you do you will have another god besides Him. Next I must inform you that your father and your mother are well, but I am troubled with one of my hips ; for now the war breaks out afresh with all that was suffered in it. What youth sows age must reap; and this is true both in regard to the mind and the body, which now throbs and pains, and tempts one to make any number of lamentations. But old age should not complain ; for wisdom flows from wounds, and pain preaches patience, that man may grow strong enough for the last journey. To-day I have taken up my pen for many reasons, and first and above all for the sake of Marit, who has become a God-fearing maiden, but who is as light of foot as a reindeer, and of rather a fickle disposition. She would be glad to abide by one thing, but is prevented from so doing by her nature; but I have often before seen that with hearts of such weak stuff the Lord is indulgent and long-suffering, and does not allow them to be tempted beyond their strength, lest they break to pieces, for she is very fragile. I duly gave her your letter, and she hid it from all save her own heart. If God will lend His aid in this matter, I have nothing against it, for Marit is most charming to young men, as plainly can be seen, and she has abundance of earthly goods, and the heavenly ones she has too, with all her fickleness. For the fear of God in her mind is like water in a shallow pond: it is there when it rains, but it is gone when the sun shines.

My eyes can endure no more at present, for they see well at a distance, but pain me and fill with tears when I look at small objects. In conclusion, I will advise you, Öyvind, to have your God with you in all your desires and undertakings, for it is written : " Better is an

handful with quietness, than both the hands
full with travail and vexation of spirit." Ec-
clesiastes, iv. 6.   Your old school-master,

Baard Andersen Opdal.

To the most Honored Maiden, Marit Knudsdatter Heidegards : —

You have my thanks for your letter, which
I have read and burned, as you requested. You
write of many things, but not at all concerning
that of which I wanted you to write. Nor do
I dare write anything definite before I know
how you are in *every respect*. The school-master's letter says nothing that one can depend
on, but he praises you and he says you are fickle.
That, indeed, you were before. Now I do not
know what to think, and so you must write, for
it will not be well with me until you do. Just
now I remember best about your coming to the
cliff that last evening and what you said then.
I will say no more this time, and so farewell.

Most respectfully,

Öyvind Pladsen.

To Öyvind Thoresen Pladsen : —

The school-master has given me another letter from you, and I have just read it, but I do
not understand it in the least, and that, I dare

say, is because I am not learned. You want to know how it is with me in every respect; and I am healthy and well, and there is nothing at all the matter with me. I eat heartily, especially when I get milk porridge. I sleep at night, and occasionally in the day-time too. I have danced a great deal this winter, for there have been many parties here, and that has been very pleasant. I go to church when the snow is not too deep; but we have had a great deal of snow this winter. Now, I presume, you know everything, and if you do not, I can think of nothing better than for you to write to me once more.

MARIT KNUDSDATTER.

TO THE MOST HONORED MAIDEN, MARIT KNUDSDAT TER HEIDEGARDS :—

I have received your letter, but you seem inclined to leave me no wiser than I was before. Perhaps this may be meant for an answer. I do not know. I dare not write anything that I wish to write, for I do not know you. But possibly you do not know me either.

You must not think that I am any longer the soft cheese you squeezed the water away from when I sat watching you dance. I have laid on many shelves to dry since that time. Neither am I like those long-haired dogs who drop their ears at the least provocation and take flight from people, as in former days. I can stand fire now.

Your letter was very playful, but it jested where it should not have jested at all, for you understood me very well, and you could see that I did not ask in sport, but because of late I can think of nothing else than the subject I questioned you about. I was waiting in deep anxiety, and there came to me only foolery and laughter.

Farewell, Marit Heidegards, I shall not look at you too much, as I did at that dance. May you both eat well, and sleep well, and get your new web finished, and above all, may you be able to shovel away the snow which lies in front of the church-door.

Most respectfully,
ÖYVIND THORESEN PLADSEN.

To the Agriculturist, Öyvind Thoresen, at the Agricultural School : —

Notwithstanding my advanced years, and the weakness of my eyes, and the pain in my right hip, I must yield to the importunity of the young, for we old people are needed by them when they have caught themselves in some snare. They entice us and weep until they are set free, but then at once run away from us again, and will take no further advice.

Now it is Marit; she coaxes me with many sweet words to write at the same time she does, for she takes comfort in not writing alone. I have read your letter; she thought that she had Jon Hatlen or some other fool to deal with, and not one whom school-master Baard had trained; but now she is in a dilemma. However, you have been too severe, for there are certain women who take to jesting in order to avoid weeping, and who make no difference between the two. But it pleases me to have you take serious things seriously, for otherwise you could not laugh at nonsense.

Concerning the feelings of both, it is now apparent from many things that you are bent on having each other. About Marit I have often been in doubt, for she is like the wind's course; but I have now learned that notwith-standing this she has resisted Jon Hatlen's advances, at which her grandfather's wrath is sorely kindled. She was happy when your offer came, and if she jested it was from joy, not from any harm. She has endured much, and has done so in order to wait for him on whom her mind was fixed. And now you will not have her, but cast her away as you would a naughty child.

This was what I wanted to tell you. And this counsel I must add, that you should come to an understanding with her, for you can find enough else to be at variance with. I am like the old man who has lived through three generations; I have seen folly and its course.

Your mother and father send love by me. They are expecting you home; but I would not write of this before, lest you should become homesick. You do not know your father; he is like a tree which makes no moan until it is hewn down. But if ever any mischance should befall you, then you will learn to know him, and you will wonder at the richness of his nature. He has had heavy burdens to bear, and is silent in worldly matters; but your mother has relieved his mind from earthly anxiety, and now daylight is beginning to break through the gloom.

Now my eyes grow dim, my hand refuses to do more. Therefore I commend you to Him whose eye ever watches, and whose hand is never weary.

BAARD ANDERSEN OPDAL.

To ÖYVIND PLADSEN: —

You seem to be displeased with me, and this greatly grieves me. For I did not mean to make you angry. I meant well. I know I have often failed to do rightly by you, and that is why I write to you now; but you must not show the letter to any one. Once I had everything just as I desired, and then I was not kind; but now there is no one who cares for me, and I am very wretched. Jon Hatlen has made a lampoon about me, and all the boys sing it, and I no longer dare go to the dances. Both the old people know about it, and I have to listen to many harsh words. Now I am sitting alone writing, and you must not show my letter.

You have learned much and are able to advise me, but you are now far away. I have often been down to see your parents, and have talked with your mother, and we have become good friends; but I did not like to say anything about it, for you wrote so strangely. The school-master only makes fun of me, and he knows nothing about the lampoon, for no one in the parish would presume to sing such a thing to him. I stand alone now, and have no one to speak with. I remember when we were children, and you were so kind to me; and I always sat on your sled, and I could wish that I were a child again.

I cannot ask you to answer me, for I dare not do so. But if you will answer just once more I will never forget it in you, Öyvind.

MARIT KNUDSDATTER.

Please burn this letter; I scarcely know whether I dare send it.

DEAR MARIT, — Thank you for your letter; you wrote it in a lucky hour. I will tell you now, Marit, that I love you so much that I can scarcely wait here any longer; and if you love me as truly in return all the lampoons of Jon and harsh words of others shall be like leaves which grow too plentifully on the tree. Since I received your letter I feel like a new being, for double my former strength has come to me, and I fear no one in the whole world. After I had sent my last letter I regretted it so that I almost became ill. And now you shall hear what the result of this was. The superintendent took me aside and asked what was the matter with me; he fancied I was studying too hard. Then he told me that when my year was out I might remain here one more, without expense. I could help him with sundry things, and he would teach me more. Then I thought that work was the only thing I had to rely on, and I thanked him very much; and I do not yet repent it, although now I long for you, for the longer I stay here the better right I shall have to ask for you one day. How happy I am now! I work like three people, and never will I be behind-hand in any work! But you must have a book that I am reading, for there is much in it about love. I read in it in the evening when the others are sleeping, and then I read your letter over again. Have you thought about our meeting? I think of it so often, and you, too, must try and find out how delightful it will be. I am truly happy that I have toiled and studied so much, although it was hard before; for now I can say what I please to you, and smile over it in my heart.

I shall give you many books to read, that you may see how much tribulation they have borne who have truly loved each other, and that they would rather die of grief than forsake each other. And that is what we would do, and do it with the greatest joy. True, it will be nearly two years before we see each other, and still longer before we get each other; but with every day that passes there is one day less to wait; we must think of this while we are working.

My next letter shall be about many things ,
but this evening I have no more paper, and the
others are asleep. Now I will go to bed and
think of you, and I will do so until I fall asleep

Your friend,

ÖYVIND PLADSEN.

CHAPTER IX.

ONE Saturday, in midsummer, Thore Pladsen rowed across the lake to meet his son, who
was expected to arrive that afternoon from the
agricultural school, where he had finished his
course. The mother had hired women several
days beforehand, and everything was scoured
and clean. The bedroom had been put in order
some time before, a stove had been set up, and
there Öyvind was to be. To-day the mother
carried in fresh greens, laid out clean linen,
made up the bed, and all the while kept looking out to see if, perchance, any boat were
coming across the lake. A plentiful table was
spread in the house, and there was always
something wanting, or flies to chase away, and
the bedroom was dusty, — continually dusty.
Still no boat came. The mother leaned against
the window and looked across the waters ; then
she heard a step near at hand on the road, and
turned her head. It was the school-master,
who was coming slowly down the hill, support-
ing himself on a staff, for his hip troubled him.

His intelligent eyes looked calm. He paused to rest, and nodded to her : —

" Not come yet ? "

" No ; I expect them every moment."

" Fine weather for haymaking, to-day."

" But warm for old folks to be walking."

The school-master looked at her, smiling, —

" Have any young folks been out to-day ? "

" Yes ; but are gone again."

" Yes, yes, to be sure ; there will most likely be a meeting somewhere this evening."

" I presume there will be. Thore says they shall not meet in his house until they have the old man's consent."

" Right, quite right."

Presently the mother cried, —

" There ! I think they are coming."

The school-master looked long in the distance.

" Yes, indeed ! it is they."

The mother left the window, and he went into the house. After he had rested a little and taken something to drink, they proceeded down to the shore, while the boat darted toward them, making rapid headway, for both father and son were rowing. The oarsmen had thrown off their jackets, the waters whitened beneath their strokes ; and so the boat soor

drew near those who were waiting. Öyvind
turned his head and looked up; he saw the two
at the landing-place, and resting his oars, he
shouted, —

"Good-day, mother! Good-day, school-master!"

"What a manly voice he has," said the
mother, her face sparkling. "O dear, O dear!
he is as fair as ever," she added.

The school-master drew in the boat. The
father laid down his oars, Öyvind sprang past
him and out of the boat, shook hands first with
his mother, then with the school-master. He
laughed and laughed again; and, quite contrary
to the custom of peasants, immediately began
to pour out a flood of words about the examination, the journey, the superintendent's certifi-
cate, and good offers; he inquired about the
crops and his acquaintances, all save one. The
father had paused to carry things up from the
boat, but, wanting to hear, too, thought they
might remain there for the present, and joined
the others. And so they walked up toward the
house, Öyvind laughing and talking, the mother
laughing, too, for she was utterly at a loss to
know what to say. The school-master moved
slowly along at Öyvind's side, watching his old
pupil closely; the father walked at a respect-

ful distance. And thus they reached home. Öyvind was delighted with everything he saw: first because the house was painted, then because the mill was enlarged, then because the leaden windows had been taken out in the family-room and in the bed-chamber, and white glass had taken the place of green, and the window frames had been made larger. When he entered everything seemed astonishingly small, and not at all as he remembered it, but very cheerful. The clock cackled like a fat hen, the carved chairs almost seemed as if they would speak; he knew every dish on the table spread before him, the freshly white-washed hearth smiled welcome; the greens, decorating the walls, scattered about them their fragrance, the juniper, strewn over the floor, gave evidence of the festival.

They all sat down to the meal; but there was not much eaten, for Öyvind rattled away without ceasing. The others viewed him now more composedly, and observed in what respect he had altered, in what he remained unchanged; looked at what was entirely new about him, even to the blue broadcloth suit he wore. Once when he had been telling a long story about one of his companions and finally concluded, as there was a little pause, the father said, —

" I scarcely understand a word that you say, boy ; you talk so very fast."

They all laughed heartily, and Öyvind not the least. He knew very well this was true, but it was not possible for him to speak more slowly. Everything new he had seen and learned, during his long absence from home, had so affected his imagination and understanding, and had so driven him out of his accustomed demeanor, that faculties which long had lain dormant were roused up, as it were, and his brain was in a state of constant activity. Moreover, they observed that he had a habit of arbitrarily taking up two or three words here and there, and repeating them again and again from sheer haste. He seemed to be stumbling over himself. Sometimes this appeared absurd, but then he laughed and it was forgotten. The school-master and the father sat watching to see if any of the old thoughtfulness was gone ; but it did not seem so. Öyvind remembered everything, and was even the one to remind the others that the boat should be unloaded. He unpacked his clothes at once and hung them up, displayed his books, his watch, everything new, and all was well cared for, his mother said. He was exceedingly pleased with his little room. He would remain at home for the present, he

said, — help with the hay-making, and study.
Where he should go later he did not know;
but it made not the least difference to him. He
had acquired a briskness and vigor of thought
which it did one good to see, and an animation
in the expression of his feelings which is so
refreshing to a person who the whole year
through strives to repress his own. The school-
master grew ten years younger.

"Now we have come *so far* with him," said
he, beaming with satisfaction as he rose to go.

When the mother returned from waiting on
him, as usual, to the door-step, she called Öyvind into the bedroom.

"Some one will be waiting for you at nine
o'clock," whispered she.

" Where ? "

" On the cliff."

Öyvind glanced at the clock; it was nearly
nine. He could not wait in the house, but
went out, clambered up the side of the cliff,
paused on the top, and looked around. The
house lay directly below; the bushes on the
roof had grown large, all the young trees round
about him had also grown, and he recognized
every one of them. His eyes wandered down
the road, which ran along the cliff, and was
bordered by the forest on the other side. The

road lay there, gray and solemn, but the forest was enlivened with varied foliage; the trees were tall and well grown. In the little bay lay a boat with unfurled sail; it was laden with planks and awaiting a breeze. Öyvind gazed across the water which had borne him away and home again. There it stretched before him, calm and smooth; some sea-birds flew over it, but made no noise, for it was late. His father came walking up from the mill, paused on the door-step, took a survey of all about him, as his son had done, then went down to the water to take the boat in for the night. The mother appeared at the side of the house, for she had been in the kitchen. She raised her eyes toward the cliff as she crossed the farm-yard with something for the hens, looked up again and began to hum. Öyvind sat down to wait. The underbrush was so dense that he could not see very far into the forest, but he listened to the slightest sound. For a long time he heard nothing but the birds that flew up and cheated him, — after a while a squirrel that was leaping from tree to tree. But at length there was a rustling farther off; it ceased a moment, and then began again. He rises, his heart throbs, the blood rushes to his head; then something breaks through the brushes close by him; but

it is a large, shaggy dog, which, on seeing him,
pauses on three legs without stirring. It is the
dog from the Upper Heidegards, and close behind him another rustling is heard. The dog
turns his head and wags his tail; now Marit
appears.

A bush caught her dress; she turned to
free it, and so she was standing when Öyvind
saw her first. Her head was bare, her hair
twisted up as girls usually wear it in every-day
attire; she had on a thick plaid dress without
sleeves, and nothing about the neck except a
turned-down linen collar. She had just stolen
away from work in the fields, and had not
ventured on any change of dress. Now she
looked up askance and smiled; her white teeth
shone, her eyes sparkled beneath the half-closed
lids. Thus she stood for a moment working
with her fingers, and then she came forward,
growing rosier and rosier with each step. He
advanced to meet her, and took her hand between both of his. Her eyes were fixed on the
ground, and so they stood.

"Thank you for all your letters," was the
first thing he said; and when she looked up
a little and laughed, he felt that she was the
most roguish troll he could meet in a wood;
but he was captured, and she, too, was evidently caught.

"How tall you have grown," said she, meaning something quite different.

She looked at him more and more, laughed more and more, and he laughed, too; but they said nothing. The dog had seated himself on the slope, and was surveying the gard. Thore observed the dog's head from the water, but could not for his life understand what it could be that was showing itself on the cliff above.

But the two had now let go of each other's hands and were beginning to talk a little. And when Öyvind was once under way he burst into such a rapid stream of words that Marit had to laugh at him.

"Yes, you see, this is the way it is when I am happy — truly happy, you see; and as soon as it was settled between us two, it seemed as if there burst open a lock within me — wide open, you see."

She laughed. Presently she said, —

"I know almost by heart all the letters you sent me."

"And I yours! But you always wrote such short ones."

"Because you always wanted them to be so long."

"And when I desired that we should write more about something, then you changed the subject."

"'I show to the best advantage when you see my tail,'[1] said the hulder."

"Ah! that is so. You have never told me how you got rid of Jon Hatlen."

"I laughed."

"How?"

"Laughed. Do not you know what it is to laugh?"

"Yes; I can laugh."

"Let me see!"

"Whoever heard of such a thing! Surely, I must have something to laugh at."

"I do not need that when I am happy."

"Are you happy now, Marit?"

"Pray, am I laughing now?"

"Yes; you are, indeed."

---

[1] The hulder in the Norse folk-lore appears like a beautiful woman, and usually wears a blue petticoat and a white sword; but she unfortunately has a long tail, like a cow's, which she anxiously strives to conceal when she is among people. She is fond of cattle, particularly brindled, of which she possesses a beautiful and thriving stock. They are without horns. She was once at a merry-making, where every one was desirous of dancing with the handsome, strange damsel; but in the midst of the mirth a young man, who had just begun a dance with her, happened to cast his eye on her tail. Immediately guessing whom he had gotten for a partner, he was not a little terrified; but, collecting himself, and unwilling to betray her, he merely said to her when the dance was over: "Fair maid, you will lose your garter." She instantly vanished, but afterwards rewarded the silent and considerate youth with beautiful presents and a good breed of cattle. FAYE's *Traditions.* — NOTE BY TRANSLATOR.

He took both her hands in his and clapped them together over and over again, gazing into her face. Here the dog began to growl, then his hair bristled and he fell to barking at something below, growing more and more savage, and finally quite furious. Marit sprang back in alarm; but Öyvind went forward and looked down. It was his father the dog was barking at. He was standing at the foot of the cliff with both hands in his pockets, gazing at the dog.

"Are you there, you two? What mad dog is that you have up there?"

"It is the dog from the Heidegards," answered Öyvind, somewhat embarrassed.

"How the deuce did it get up there?"

Now the mother had put her head out of the kitchen door, for she had heard the dreadful noise, and at once knew what it meant; and laughing, she said, —

"That dog is roaming about there every day, so there is nothing remarkable in it."

"Well, I must say it is a fierce dog."

"It will behave better if I stroke it," thought Öyvind, and he did so.

The dog stopped barking, but growled. The father walked away as though he knew nothing, and the two on the cliff were saved from discovery.

"It was all right this time," said Marit, as they drew near to each other again.

"Do you expect it to be worse hereafter?"

"I know one who will keep a close watch on us — that I do."

"Your grandfather?"

"Yes, indeed."

"But he shall do us no harm."

"Not the least."

"And you promise that?"

"Yes, I promise it, Öyvind."

"How beautiful you are, Marit!"

"So the fox said to the raven and got the cheese."

"I mean to have the cheese, too, I can assure you."

"You shall not have it."

"But I will take it."

She turned her head, but he did not take it.

"I can tell you one thing, Öyvind, though."
She looked up sideways as she spoke.

"Well?"

"How homely you have grown!"

"Ah! you are going to give me the cheese, anyway; are you?"

"No, I am not," and she turned away again.

"Now I must go, Öyvind."

"I will go with you."

"But not beyond the woods; grandfather might see you."

"No, not beyond the woods. Dear me! are you running?"

"Why, we cannot walk side by side here."

"But this is not going together?"

"Catch me, then!"

She ran; he after her; and soon she was fast in the bushes, so that he overtook her.

"Have I caught you forever, Marit?" His hand was on her waist.

"I think so," said she, and laughed; but she was both flushed and serious.

"Well, now is the time," thought he, and he made a movement to kiss her; but she bent her head down under his arm, laughed, and ran away. She paused, though, by the last trees.

"And when shall we meet again?" whispered she.

"To-morrow, to-morrow!" he whispered in return.

"Yes; to-morrow."

"Good-by," and she ran on.

"Marit!" She stopped. "Say, was it not strange that we met first on the cliff?"

"Yes, it was." She ran on again.

Öyvind gazed long after her. The dog ran on before her, barking; Marit followed, quiet ing him. Öyvind turned, took off his cap and tossed it into the air, caught it, and threw it up again.

" Now I really think I am beginning to be happy," said the boy, and went singing homeward.

CHAPTER X.

ONE afternoon later in the summer, as his mother and a girl were raking hay, while Öyvind and his father were carrying it in, there came a little barefooted and bareheaded boy, skipping down the hill-side and across the meadows to Öyvind, and gave him a note.

"You run well, my boy," said Öyvind.

"I am paid for it," answered the boy.

On being asked if he was to have an answer, the reply was No; and the boy took his way home over the cliff, for some one was coming after him up on the road, he said. Öyvind opened the note with some difficulty, for it was folded in a strip, then tied in a knot, then sealed and stamped; and the note ran thus:—

"He is now on the march; but he moves slowly. Run into the woods and hide yourself! THE ONE YOU KNOW."

"I will do no such thing," thought Öyvind; and gazed defiantly up the hills. Nor did he wait long before an old man appeared on the hill-top, paused to rest, walked on a little, rested again. Both Thore and his wife stopped to look. Thore soon smiled, however; his wife, on the other hand, changed color.

" Do you know him ? "

" Yes, it is not very easy to make a mistake here."

Father and son again began to carry hay; but the latter took care that they were always together. The old man on the hill slowly drew near, like a heavy western storm. He was very tall and rather corpulent; he was lame and walked with a labored gait, leaning on a staff. Soon he came so near that they could see him distinctly; he paused, removed his cap and wiped away the perspiration with a handkerchief. He was quite bald far back on the head; he had a round, wrinkled face, small, glittering, blinking eyes, bushy eyebrows, and had lost none of his teeth. When he spoke it was in a sharp, shrill voice, that seemed to be hopping over gravel and stones; but it lingered on an " r " here and there with great satisfaction, rolling it over for several yards, and at the same time making a tremendous leap in pitch. He had been known in his younger days as a lively but quick-tempered man ; in his old age, through much adversity, he had become irritable and suspicious.

Thore and his son came and went many times before Ole could make his way to them; they both know that he did not come for any good purpose, therefore it was all the more comical that he never got there. Both had to walk very serious, and talk in a whisper; but as this did not come to an end it became ludicrous. Only half a word that is to the point can kindle laughter under such circumstances, and especially when it is dangerous to laugh. When at last Ole was only a few rods distant, but which seemed never to grow less, Öyvind said, dryly, in a low tone, —

"He must carry a heavy load, that man," — and more was not required.

"I think you are not very wise," whispered the father, although he was laughing himself.

"Hem, hem!" said Ole, coughing on the hill.

"He is getting his throat ready," whispered Thore.

Öyvind fell on his knees in front of the haycock, buried his head in the hay, and laughed. His father also bowed down.

"Suppose we go into the barn," whispered he, and taking an armful of hay he trotted off. Öyvind picked up a little tuft, rushed after him, bent crooked with laughter, and dropped down as soon as he was inside the barn. His father was a grave man, but if he once got to laughing, there first began within him a low chuckling, with an occasional ha-ha-ha, gradually growing longer and longer, until all blended in a single loud peal, after which came wave after wave with a longer gasp between each. Now he was under way. The son lay on the floor, the father stood beside him, both laughing with all their might. Occasionally they had such fits of laughter.

" But this is inconvenient," said the father.

Finally they were at a loss to know how this would end, for the old man must surely have reached the gard.

"I will not go out," said the father; "I have no business with him."

" Well, then, I will not go out either," replied Öyvind.

" Hem, hem ! " was heard just outside of the barn wall.

The father held up a threatening finger to his boy.

" Come, out with you ! "

" Yes ; you go first ! "

" No, you be off at once."

" Well, go you first."

And they brushed the dust off each other

and advanced very seriously. When they came
below the barn-bridge they saw Ole standing
with his face towards the kitchen door, as if
he were reflecting. He held his cap in the
same hand as his staff, and with his handkerchief was wiping the sweat from his bald head,
at the same time pulling at the bushy tufts
behind his ears and about his neck until they
stuck out like spikes. Öyvind hung behind
his father, so the latter was obliged to stand
still, and in order to put an end to this he said
with excessive gravity, —

" Is the old gentleman out for a walk ? "

Ole turned, looked sharply at him, and put
on his cap before he replied, —

" Yes, so it seems."

" Perhaps you are tired; will you not walk
in ? "

" Oh ! I can rest very well here ; my errand
will not take long."

Some one set the kitchen door ajar and looked
out ; between it and Thore stood old Ole, with
his cap-visor down over his eyes, for the cap
was too large now that he had lost his hair. In
order to be able to see he threw his head pretty
far back ; he held his staff in his right hand,
while the left was firmly pressed against his
side when he was not gesticulating ; and this

he never did more vigorously than by stretch-
ing the hand half way out and holding it pas-
sive a moment, as a guard for his dignity.

" Is that your son who is standing behind
you ? " he began, abruptly.

" So they say."

" Öyvind is his name, is it not ? "

" Yes ; they call him Öyvind."

" He has been at one of those agricultural
schools down south, I believe ? "

" There was something of the kind ; yes."

" Well, my girl — she — my granddaughter
— Marit, you know — she has gone mad of
late."

" That is too bad."

" She refuses to marry."

" Well, really ? "

" She will not have any of the gard boys who
offer themselves."

" Ah, indeed."

" But people say he is to blame ; he who is
standing there."

" Is that so ? "

" He is said to have turned her head — yes ;
he there, your son Öyvind."

" The deuce he has ! "

" See you, I do not like to have any one take
my horses when I let them loose on the mount-

ains, neither do I choose to have any one take
my daughters when I allow them to go to a
dance. I will not have it."

"No, of course not."

"I cannot go with them; I am old, I cannot
be forever on the lookout."

"No, no! no, no!"

"Yes, you see, I will have order and pro-
priety; there the block must stand, and there
the axe must lie, and there the knife, and there
they must sweep, and there throw rubbish out,
— not outside the door, but yonder in the corner, just there — yes; and nowhere else. So,
when I say to her: 'not this one but that one!'
I expect it to be that one, and not this one!"

"Certainly."

"But it is not so. For three years she has
persisted in thwarting me, and for three years
we have not been happy together. This is
bad; and if he is at the bottom of it, I will
tell him so that you may hear it, you, his father, that it will not do him any good. He
may as well give it up."

"Yes, yes."

Ole looked a moment at Thore, then he
said, —

"Your answers are short."

"A sausage is no longer."

Here Öyvind had to laugh, although he was
in no mood to do so. But with daring persons
fear always borders on laughter, and now it inclined to the latter.

" What are you laughing at? " asked Ole
shortly and sharply.

" I ? "

" Are you laughing at me? "

" The Lord forbid ! " but his own answer increased his desire to laugh.

Ole saw this, and grew absolutely furious.
Both Thore and Öyvind tried to make amends
with serious faces and entreaties to walk in ; but
it was the pent-up wrath of three years that
was now seeking vent, and there was no check-
ing it.

" You need not think you can make a fool of
me," he began ; " I am on a lawful errand : I
am protecting my grandchild's happiness, as I
understand it, and puppy laughter shall not
hinder me. One does not bring up girls to
toss them down into the first houseman's place
that opens its doors, and one does not manage
an estate for forty years only to hand the whole
over to the first one who makes a fool of the
girl. My daughter made herself ridiculous un
til she was allowed to marry a vagabond. He
drank them both into the grave, and I had to

take the child and pay for the fun; but, by my
troth! it shall not be the same with my granddaughter, and now you know *that!* I tell you,
as sure as my name is Ole Nordistuen of the
Heidegards, the priest shall sooner publish the
bans of the hulder-folks up in the Nordal forest than give out such names from the pulpit
as Marit's and yours, you Christmas clown!
Do you think you are going to drive respect-
able suitors away from the gard, forsooth?
Well; you just try to come there, and you
shall have such a journey down the hills that
your shoes will come after you like smoke.
You snickering fox! I suppose you have a no-
tion that I do not know what you are thinking
of, both you and she. Yes, you think that old
Ole Nordistuen will turn his nose to the skies
yonder, in the churchyard, and then you will
trip forward to the altar. No; I have lived
now sixty-six years, and I will prove to you,
boy, that I shall live until you waste away over
it, both of you! I can tell you this, too, that
you may cling to the house like new-fallen
snow, yet not so much as see the soles of her
feet; for I mean to send her from the parish.
I am going to send her where she will be safe;
so you may flutter about here like a chattering
jay all you please, and marry the rain and the

north wind. This is all I have to say to you ,
but now you, who are his father, know my sen-
timents, and if you desire the welfare of him
whom this concerns, you had better advise him
to lead the stream where it can find its course ;
across my possessions it is forbidden."

He turned away with short, hasty steps, lifting his right foot rather higher than the left,
and grumbling to himself.

Those left behind were completely sobered ;
a foreboding of evil had become blended with
their jesting and laughter, and the house
seemed, for a while, as empty as after a great
fright. The mother who, from the kitchen
door had heard everything, anxiously sought
Öyvind's eyes, scarcely able to keep back her
tears, but she would not make it harder for
him by saying a single word. After they had
all silently entered the house, the father sat
down by the window, and gazed out after Ole,
with much earnestness in his face; Öyvind's
eyes hung on the slightest change of counte-
nance; for on his father's first words almost
depended the future of the two young people.
If Thore united his refusal with Ole's, it could
scarcely be overcome. Öyvind's thoughts flew,
terrified, from obstacle to obstacle; for a time
he saw only poverty, opposition, misunderstand-

ing, and a sense of wounded honor, and every prop he tried to grasp seemed to glide away from him. It increased his uneasiness that his mother was standing with her hand on the latch of the kitchen-door, uncertain whether she had the courage to remain inside and await the issue, and that she at last lost heart entirely and stole out. Öyvind gazed fixedly at his father, who never took his eyes from the window; the son did not dare speak, for the other must have time to think the matter over fully. But at the same moment his soul had fully run its course of anxiety, and regained its poise once more. "No one but God can part us in the end," he thought to himself, as he looked at his father's wrinkled brow. Soon after this something occurred. Thore drew a long sigh, rose, glanced round the room, and met his son's gaze. He paused, and looked long at him.

"It was my will that you should give her up, for one should hesitate about succeeding through entreaties or threats. But if you are determined not to give her up, you may let me know when the opportunity comes, and perhaps I can help you."

He started off to his work, and the son followed.

But that evening Öyvind had his plan

formed : he would endeavor to become agriculturist for the district, and ask the inspector and the school-master to aid him. " If she only remains firm, with God's help, I shall win her through my work."

He waited in vain for Marit that evening, but as he walked about he sang his favorite song : —

"Hold thy head up, thou eager boy!
Time a hope or two may destroy,
Soon in thy eye thongh is gleaming,
Light that above thee is beaming!

"Hold thy head up, and gaze about!
Something thon 'lt find that " Come!" does shout
Thousands of tongues it has bringing
Tidings of peace with their singing.

"Hold thy head up; within thee, too,
Rises a mighty vault of blue,
Wherein are harp tones sounding,
Swinging, exulting, rebounding.

"Hold thy head up, and londly sing!
Keep not back what would sprout in spring
Powers fermenting, glowing,
Must find a time for growing.

"Hold thy head up; baptism take,
From the hope that on high does break,
Arches of light o'er us throwing,
And in each life-spark glowing." [1]

[1] Auber Forestier's translation.

CHAPTER XI.

IT was during the noonday rest; the people at the great Heidegards were sleeping, the hay was scattered over the meadows, the rakes were staked in the ground. Below the barn-bridge stood the hay sleds, the harness lay, taken off, beside them, and the horses were tethered at a little distance. With the exception of the latter and some hens that had strayed across the fields, not a living creature was visible on the whole plain.

There was a notch in the mountains above the gards, and through it the road led to the Heidegard sæters, — large, fertile mountain plains. A man was standing in this notch, taking a survey of the plain below, just as if he were watching for some one. Behind him lay a little mountain lake, from which flowed the brook which made this mountain pass; on either side of this lake ran cattle-paths, lead-.ng to the sæters, which could be seen in the distance. There floated toward him a shout-ing and a barking, cattle-bells tinkled among

the mountain ridges; for the cows had strag
gled apart in search of water, and the dogs and
herd-boys were vainly striving to drive them
together.   The cows came galloping along with
the most absurd antics and involuntary plunges,
and with short, mad bellowing, their tails held
aloft, they rushed down into the water, where
they came to a stand ; every time they moved
their heads the tinkling of their bells was heard
across the lake.   The dogs drank a little, but
stayed behind on firm land; the herd-boys followed, and seated themselves on the warm,
smooth hill-side.   Here they drew forth their
lunch boxes, exchanged with one another,
bragged about their dogs, oxen, and the family
they lived with, then undressed, and sprang
into the water with the cows.   The dogs persisted in not going in; but loitered lazily
around, their heads hanging, with hot eyes and
lolling tongues.   Round about on the slopes
not a bird was to be seen, not a sound was
heard, save the prattling of children and the
tinkling of bells; the heather was parched and
dry, the sun blazed on the hill-sides, so that
everything was scorched by its heat.

It was Öyvind who was sitting up there
in the mid-day sun, waiting.   He sat in his
shirt-sleeves, close by the brook which flowed

from the lake. No one yet appeared on the
Heidegard plain, and he was gradually beginning to grow anxious when suddenly a large
dog came walking with heavy steps out of a
door in Nordistuen, followed by a girl in white
sleeves. She tripped across the meadow toward the cliff; he felt a strong desire to shout
down to her, but dared not. He took a careful
survey of the gard to see if any one might
come out and notice her, but there seemed to
be no danger of detection, and several times
he rose from impatience.

She arrived at last, following a path by the
side of the brook, the dog a little in advance
of her, snuffing the air, she catching hold of the
low shrubs, and walking with more and more
weary gait. Öyvind sprang downward; the
dog growled and was hushed; but as soon as
Marit saw Öyvind coming she sat down on a
large stone, as red as blood, tired and overcome by the heat. He flung himself down on
the stone by her side.

"Thank you for coming."

"What heat and what a distance! Have
you been here long?"

"No. Since we are watched in the evening,
we must make use of the noon. But after this
I think we will not act so secretly, nor take so

much trouble ; it was just about this I wanted
to speak to you."

" Not so secretly ? "

" I know very well that all that is done secretly pleases you best ; but to show courage
pleases you also.   To-day I have come to have
a long talk with you, and now you must listen."

" Is it true that you are trying to be agriculturist for the district ? "

" Yes, and I expect to succeed.   In this I
have a double purpose : first, to win a position
for myself ; but secondly, and chiefly, to accom-
plish something which your grandfather can see
and understand.   Luckily it chances that most
of the Heidegard freeholders are young people
who wish for improvements and desire help ,
they have money, too.   So I shall begin among
them.   I shall regulate everything from their
stables to their water-pipes ; I shall give lect-
ures and work ; I shall fairly besiege the old
man with good deeds."

" Those are brave words.   What more, Öyvind ? "

" Why, the rest simply concerns us two.
You must not go away."

" Not if he orders it ? "

" And keep nothing secret that concerns us
two."

" Even if he torments me ? "

" We gain more and defend ourselves better by allowing everything to be open. We must manage to be so constantly before the eyes of people, that they are constantly forced to talk about how fond we are of each other; so much the sooner will they wish that all may go well with us. You must not leave home. There is danger of gossip forcing its way between those who are parted. We pay no heed to any idle talk the first year, but we begin by degrees to believe in it the second. We two will meet once a week and laugh away the mischief people would like to make between us; we shall be able to meet occasionally at a dance, and keep step together until everything sings about us, while those who backbite us are sitting around. We shall meet at church and greet each other so that it may attract the attention of all those who wish us a hundred miles apart. If any one makes a song about us we will sit down together and try to get up one in answer to it, we must succeed if we assist each other. No one can harm us if we keep together, and thus *show* people that we keep together. All unhappy love belongs either to timid people, or weak people, or sick people, or calculating people, who keep waiting for some special oppor

tunity, or cunning people, who, in the end,
smart for their own cunning; or to sensuous
people that do not care enough for each other
to forget rank and distinction; they go and hide
from sight, they send letters, they tremble at a
word, and finally they mistake fear, that constant uneasiness and irritation in the blood, for
love, become wretched and dissolve like sugar.
Oh pshaw! if they truly loved each other they
would have no fear; they would laugh, and
would openly march to the church door, in the
face of every smile and every word. I have
read about it in books, and I have seen it for
myself. That is a pitiful love which chooses a
secret course. Love naturally begins in secresy
because it begins in shyness; but it must live
openly because it lives in joy. It is as when
the leaves are changing; that which is to grow
cannot conceal itself, and in every instance you
see that all which is dry falls from the tree the
moment the new leaves begin to sprout. He
who gains love casts off all the old, dead rubbish he formerly clung to, the sap wells up and
rushes onward; and should no one notice it
then? Hey, my girl! they shall become happy
at seeing us happy; two who are betrothed and
remain true to each other confer a benefit on
people, for they give them a poem which their

children learn by heart to the shame of their unbelieving parents. I have read of many such cases; and some still live in the memory of the people of this parish, and those who relate these stories, and are moved by them, are the children of the very persons who once caused all the mischief. Yes, Marit, now we two will join hands, so; yes, and we will promise each other to cling together, so; yes, and now it will all come right. Hurrah!"

He was about to take hold of her head, but she turned it away and glided down off the stone.

He kept his seat; she came back, and leaning her arms on his knee, stood talking with him, looking up into his face.

Listen, Öyvind; what if he is determined I shall leave home, how then?"

"Then you must say No, right out."

"Oh, dear! how would that be possible?"

"He cannot carry you out to the carriage."

"If he does not quite do that, he can force me in many other ways."

"That I do not believe; you owe obedience, to be sure, as long as it is not a sin; but it is also your duty to let him fully understand how hard it is for you to be obedient this time. I am sure he will change his mind when he sees

this; now he thinks, like most people, that it is
only childish nonsense. Prove to him that it is
something more."

" He is not to be trifled with, I can assure
you. He watches me like a tethered goat."

" But you tug at the tether several times a
day."

" That is not true."

" Yes, you do; every time you think of me
in secret you tug at it."

" Yes, in that way. But are you so very
sure that I think often of you ? "

" You would not be sitting here if you did
not."

" Why, dear me ! did you not send word for
me to come? "

" But you came because your thoughts drove
you here."

" Rather because the weather was so fine."

" You said a while ago that it was too warm.'

" To go *up* hill, yes ; but *down* again ? "

" Why did you come up, then ? "

" That I might run down again."

" Why did you not run down before this ? "

" Because I had to rest."

" And talk with me about love? "

" It was an easy matter to give you the pleasure of listening."

" While the birds sang."

" And the others were sleeping."

" And the bells rang."

" In the shady grove."

Here they both saw Marit's grandfather come sauntering out into the yard, and go to the bell-rope to ring the farm people up. The people came slowly forth from the barns, sheds, and houses, moved sleepily toward their horses and rakes, scattered themselves over the meadow, and presently all was life and work again. Only the grandfather went in and out of the houses, and finally up on the highest barn-bridge and looked out. There came running up to him a little boy, whom he must have called. The boy, sure enough, started off in the direction of Pladsen. The grandfather, meanwhile, moved about the gard, often looking upward and having a suspicion, at least, that the black spot on the " giant rock " was Marit and Öyvind. Now for the second time Marit's great dog was the cause of trouble. He saw a strange horse drive in to the Heidegards, and believing himself to be only doing his duty, began to bark with all his might. They hushed the dog, but he had grown angry and would not be quiet ; the grandfather stood below staring up. Bᵢ matters grew still worse, for all the herd-

boys' dogs heard with surprise the strange voice
and came running up. When they saw that it
was a large, wolf-like giant, all the stiff-haired
Lapp-dogs gathered about him. Marit became
so terrified that she ran away without saying
farewell. Öyvind rushed into the midst of the
fray, kicked and fought; but the dogs merely
changed the field of battle, and then flew at
one another again, with hideous howls and
kicks; Öyvind after them again, and so it kept
on until they had rolled over to the edge of
the brook, when he once more came running
up. The result of this was that they all tum-
bled together into the water, just at a place
where it was quite deep, and there they parted,
shame-faced. Thus ended this forest battle.
Öyvind walked through the forest until he
reached the parish road; but Marit met her
grandfather up by the fence. This was the
dog's fault.

" Where do you come from? "

" From the wood."

" What were you doing there? "

" Plucking berries."

" That is not true."

" No; neither is it."

" What were you doing, then? "

" I was talking with some one."

" Was it with the Pladsen boy? "

" Yes."

" Hear me now, Marit; to-morrow you leave home."

" No."

" Listen to me, Marit; I have but one single thing to say, only one: you *shall* go."

" You cannot lift me into the carriage."

" Indeed? Can I not? "

" No; because you will not."

" Will I not? Listen now, Marit, just for sport, you see, just for sport. I am going to tell you that I will crush the backbone of that worthless fellow of yours."

" No; you would not dare do so."

" I would not dare? Do you say I would not dare? Who should interfere? Who? "

" The school-master."

" School — school — school-master. Does he trouble his head about that fellow, do you think? "

" Yes; it is he who has kept him at the agricultural school."

" The school-master? "

" The school-master."

" Hearken now, Marit: I will have no more of this nonsense; you shall leave the parish. You only cause me sorrow and trouble; that

was the way with your mother, too, only sorrow and trouble. I am an old man. 1 want to
see you well provided for. I will not live in
people's talk as a fool just for this matter. I
only wish your own good; you should understand this, Marit. Soon I will be gone, and
then you will be left alone. What would have
become of your mother if it had not been for
me? Listen, Marit; be sensible, pay heed to
what I have to say. I only desire your own
good."

"No, you do not."

"Indeed? What do I want, then?"

"To carry out your own will, that is what
you want; but you do not ask about mine."

"And have you a will, you young sea-gull,
you? Do you suppose you know what is for
your good, you fool? I will give you a taste of
the rod, I will, for all you are so big and tall.
Listen now, Marit; let me talk kindly with
you. You are not so bad at heart, but you
have lost your senses. You must listen to me.
I am an old and sensible man. We will talk
kindly together a little; I have not done so
remarkably well in the world as folks think; a
poor bird on the wing could easily fly away
with the little I have; your father handled it
roughly, indeed he did. Let us care for our

selves in this world, it is the best thing we can
do. It is all very well for the school-master
to talk, for he has money himself; so has the
priest;— let them preach. But with us who
must slave for our daily bread, it is quite different. I am old. I know much. I have seen
many things; love, you see, may do very well
to talk about; yes, but it is not worth much.
It may answer for priests and such folks, peasants must look at it in a different light. First
food, you see, then God's Word, and then a
little writing and arithmetic, and then a little
love, if it happens to come in the way; but, by
the Eternals! there is no use in beginning with
love and ending with food. What can you say,
now, Marit?"

"I do not know."

" You do not know what you ought to answer?"

" Yes, indeed, I know that."

" Well, then?"

" May I say it?"

" Yes; of course you may say it."

" I care a great deal for that love of mine."

He stood aghast for a moment, recalling a
hundred similar conversations with similar re-
sults, then he shook his head, turned his back,
and walked away."

He picked a quarrel with the housemen, abused the girls, beat the large dog, and almost frightened the life out of a little hen that had strayed into the field; but to Marit he said nothing.

That evening Marit was so happy when she went up-stairs to bed, that she opened the window, lay in the window-frame, looked out and sang. She had found a pretty little love-song, and it was that she sang.

"Lovest thou but me,
　I will e'er love thee,
　All my days on earth, so fondly;
　Short were summer's days,
　Now the flower decays, —
　Comes again with spring, so kindly

"What you said last year
　Still rings in my ear,
　As I all alone am sitting,
　And your thoughts do try
　In my heart to fly, —
　Picture life in sunshine flitting

"Litli — litli — loy,
　Well I hear the boy,
　Sighs behind the birches heaving.
　I am in dismay,
　Thou must show the way,
　For the night her shroud is weaving.

"Flomma, lomma, hys,
　Sang I of a kiss,
　No, thou surely art mistaken.

Didst thou hear it, say?
Cast the thought away;
Look on me as one forsaken.

"Oh, good-night! good-night!
Dreams of eyes so bright,
Hold me now in soft embraces,
But that wily word,
Which thou thought'st unheard,
Leaves in me of love no traces.

"I my window close,
But in sweet repose
Songs from thee I hear returning;
Calling me they smile,
And my thoughts beguile, —
Must I e'er for thee be yearning?"

CHAPTER XII.

SEVERAL years have passed since the last scene.

It is well on in the autumn. The schoolmaster comes walking up to Nordistuen, opens the outer door, finds no one at home, opens another, finds no one at home; and thus he keeps on until he reaches the innermost room in the long building. There Ole Nordistuen is sitting alone, by the side of his bed, his eyes fixed on his hands.

The school-master salutes him, and receives a greeting in return; he finds a stool, and seats himself in front of Ole.

" You have sent for me," he says.

" I have."

The school-master takes a fresh quid of tobacco, glances around the room, picks up a book that is lying on the bench, and turns over the eaves.

" What did you want of me ? "

" I was just sitting here thinking it over."

The school-master gives himself plenty of

time, searches for his spectacles in order to read
the title of the book, wipes them and puts them
on.

" You are growing old, now, Ole."

" Yes, it was about that I wanted to talk
with you. I am tottering downward; I will
soon rest in the grave."

" You must see to it that you rest well there,
Ole."

He closes the book and sits looking at the
binding.

" That is a good book you are holding in
your hands."

" It is not bad. How often have you gone beyond the cover, Ole ? "

" Why, of late, I " —

The school-master lays aside the book and
puts away his spectacles.

" Things are not going as you wish to have
them, Ole ? "

" They have not done so as far back as I can
remember."

" Ah, so it was with me for a long time. I
lived at variance with a good friend, and wanted
him to come to *me*, and all the while I was unhappy. At last I took it into my head to go to
him, and since then all has been well with me."

Ole looks up and says nothing.

The school-master : " How do you think the gard is doing, Ole ? "

" Failing, like myself."

" Who shall have it when you are gone ? "

" That is what I do not know, and it is that, too, which troubles me."

" Your neighbors are doing well now, Ole."

" Yes, they have that agriculturist to help them."

The school-master turned unconcernedly toward the window : " You should have help, — you, too, Ole. You cannot walk much, and you know very little of the new ways of management."

Ole : " I do not suppose there is any one who would help me."

" Have you asked for it ? "

Ole is silent.

The school-master : " I myself dealt just so with the Lord for a long time. 'You are not kind to me,' I said to Him. 'Have you prayed me to be so ? ' asked He. No; I had not done so. Then I prayed, and since then all has been truly well with me."

Ole is silent ; but now the school-master, too, 's silent.

Finally Ole says : —

" I have a grandchild ; she knows what would

please me before I am taken away, but she does
not do it."

The school-master smiles.

" Possibly it would not please her?"

Ole makes no reply.

The school-master: " There are many things
which trouble you; but as far as I can under
stand they all concern the gard."

Ole says, quietly, —

" It has been handed down for many generations, and the soil is good. All that father after
father has toiled for lies in it; but now it does
not thrive. Nor do I know who shall drive in
when I am driven out. It will not be one of
the family."

" Your granddaughter will preserve the family."

" But how can he who takes her take the
gard? That is what I want to know before I
die. You have no time to lose, Baard, either
for me or for the gard."

They were both silent; at last the school-
master says, —

" Shall we walk out and take a look at the
gard in this fine weather?"

" Yes; let us do so. I have work-people on
the slope; they are gathering leaves, but they
do not work except when I am watching them.'

He totters off after his large cap and staff.
and says, meanwhile, —

" They do not seem to like to work for me
I cannot understand it."

When they were once out and turning the
corner of the house, he paused.

" Just look here.　No order: the wood flung
about, the axe not even stuck in the block."

He stooped with difficulty, picked up the axe,
and drove it in fast.

" Here you see a skin that has fallen down.
but has any one hung it up again ? "

He did it himself.

" And the store-house; do you think the
ladder is carried away ? "

He set it aside.　He paused, and looking at
the school-master, said, —

" This is the way it is every single day."

As they proceeded upward they heard a
merry song from the slopes.

" Why, they are singing over their work,"
said the school-master.

" That is little Knut Östistuen who is singing; he is helping his father gather leaves.
Over yonder *my* people are working; you will
not find them singing."

" That is not one of the parish songs, is it ?

" No, it is not."

"Öyvind Pladsen has been much in Östis-tuen ; perhaps that is one of the songs he has introduced into the parish, for there is always singing where he is."

There was no reply to this.

The field they were crossing was not in good condition ; it required attention. The school-master commented on this, and then Ole stopped.

" It is not in my power to do more," said he, quite pathetically. " Hired work-people with-out attention cost too much. But it is hard to walk over such a field, I can assure you."

As their conversation now turned on the size of the gard, and what portion of it most needed cultivation, they decided to go up the slope that they might have a view of the whole. When they at length had reached a high elevation, and could take it all in, the old man became moved.

" Indeed, I should not like to leave it so. We have labored hard down there, both I and those who went before me, but there is nothing to show for it."

A song rang out directly over their heads, but with the peculiar shrilling of a boy's voice when it is poured out with all its might. They were not far from the tree in whose top was perched little Knut Östistuen, gathering leaves

for his father, and they were compelled to listen
to the boy: —

" When on mountain peaks you hie,
　'Mid green slopes to tarry,
In your scrip pray no more tie,
　Than you well can carry.
Take no hindrances along
　To the crystal fountains;
Drown them in a cheerful song,
　Send them down the mountains.

" Birds there greet you from the trees,
　Gossip seeks the valley;
Purer, sweeter grows the breeze,
　As you upward sally.
Fill your lungs, and onward rove,
　Ever gayly singing,
Childhood's memories, heath and grove,
　Rosy-hued, are bringing.

" Pause the shady groves among,
　Hear yon mighty roaring,
Solitude's majestic song
　Upward far is soaring.
All the world's distraction comes
　When there rolls a pebble;
Each forgotten duty hums
　In the brooklet's treble.

" Pray, while overhead, dear heart,
　Anxious mem'ries hover;
Then go on: the better part
　You'll above discover.
Who hath chosen Christ as guide,
　Daniel and Moses,
Finds contentment far and wide,
　And in peace reposes."[1]

　　[1] Auber Forestier's translation

Ole had sat down and covered his face with his hands.

" Here I will talk witn you," said the school-master, and seated himself by his side.

Down at Pladsen, Öyvind had just returned home from a somewhat long journey, the post-boy was still at the door, as the horse was resting. Although Öyvind now had a good income as agriculturist of the district, he still lived in his little room down at Pladsen, and helped his parents every spare moment. Pladsen was cultivated from one end to the other, but it was so small that Öyvind called it "mother's toy-farm," for it was she, in particular, who saw to the farming.

He had changed his clothes, his father had come in from the mill, white with meal, and had also dressed. They just stood talking about taking a short walk before supper, when the mother came in quite pale.

" Here are singular strangers coming up to the house; oh dear! look out ! "

Both men turned to the window, and Öyvind was the first to exclaim : —

" It is the school-master, and — yes, I almost believe — why, certainly it is he ! "

" Yes, it is old Ole Nordistuen," said Thore,

moving away from the window that he might not be seen; for the two were already near the door.

Just as Öyvind was leaving the window he caught the school-master's eye, Baard smiled, and cast a glance back at old Ole, who was laboring along with his staff in small, short steps, one foot being constantly raised higher than the other. Outside the school-master was heard to say, "He has recently returned home, I suppose," and Ole to exclaim twice over, "Well, well!"

They remained a long time quiet in the passage. The mother had crept up to the corner where the milk-shelf was; Öyvind had assumed his favorite position, that is, he leaned with his back against the large table, with his face toward the door; his father was sitting near him. At length there came a knock at the door, and in stepped the school-master, who drew off his hat, afterward Ole, who pulled off his cap, and then turned to shut the door. It took him a long time to do so; he was evidently embarrassed. Thore rising, asked them to be seated; they sat down, side by side, on the bench in front of the window. Thore took his seat again.

And the wooing proceeded as shall now be told.

The school-master: "We are having fine weather this autumn, after all."

Thore: "It has been mending of late."

"It is likely to remain pleasant, now that the wind is over in that quarter."

"Are you through with your harvesting up yonder?"

"Not yet; Ole Nordistuen here, whom, perhaps, you know, would like very much to have help from you, Öyvind, if there is nothing else in the way."

Öyvind: "If help is desired, I shall do what I can."

"Well, there is no great hurry. The gard is not doing well, he thinks, and he believes what is wanting is the right kind of tillage and superintendence."

Öyvind: "I am so little at home."

The school-master looks at Ole. The latter feels that he must now rush into the fire; he clears his throat a couple of times, and begins hastily and shortly, —

"It was — it is — yes. What I meant was that you should be in a certain way established — that you should — yes — be the same as at home up yonder with us, — be there, when you were not away."

"Many thanks for the offer, but I should rather remain where I now live."

Ole looks at the school-master, who says, —

"Ole's brain seems to be in a whirl to-day. The fact is he has been here once before, and the recollection of that makes his words get all confused."

Ole, quickly: "That is it, yes; I ran a madman's race. I strove against the girl until the tree split. But let by-gones be by-gones; the wind, not the snow, beats down the grain; the rain-brook does not tear up large stones; snow does not lie long on the ground in May; it is not the thunder that kills people."

They all four laugh; the school-master says:

"Ole means that he does not want you to remember that time any longer; nor you, either, Thore."

Ole looks at them, uncertain whether he dare begin again.

Then Thore says, —

"The briar takes hold with many teeth, but causes no wound. In me there are certainly no thorns left."

Ole: "I did not know the boy then. Now I see that what he sows thrives; the harvest answers to the promise of the spring; there is money in his finger-tips, and I should like to get hold of him."

Öyvind looks at the father, he at the mother

she from them to the school-master, and then all three at the latter.

" Ole thinks that he has a large gard " —

Ole breaks in : " A large gard, but badly managed. I can do no more. I am old, and my legs refuse to run the errands of my head. But it will pay to take hold up yonder."

" The largest gard in the parish, and that by a great deal," interrupts the school-master.

" The largest gard in the parish ; that is just the misfortune ; shoes that are too large fall off ; it is a fine thing to have a good gun, but one should be able to lift it." Then turning quickly towards Öyvind, " Would you be willing to lend a hand to it ? "

" Do you mean for me to be gard overseer ?"

" Precisely — yes ; you should have the gard."

" I should *have* the gard ? "

" Just so — yes : then you could manage it."

" But " —

" You will not ? "

" Why, of course, I will."

" Yes, yes, yes, yes; then it is decided, as the hen said when she flew into the water."

" But " —

Ole looks puzzled at the school-master.

" Öyvind is asking, I suppose, whether he shall have Marit, to."

Ole, abruptly: " Marit in the bargain ; Marit in the bargain ! "

Then Öyvind burst out laughing, and jumped right up ; all three laughed with him. Öyvind rubbed his hands, paced the floor, and kept re peating again and again : " Marit in the bargain ! Marit in the bargain ! " Thore gave a deep chuckle, the mother in the corner kept her eyes fastened on her son until they filled with tears.

Ole, in great excitement : " What do you think of the gard ? "

" Magnificent land ! "

" Magnificent land ; is it not ? "

" No pasture equal to it ! "

" No pasture equal to it ! Something can be done with it ? "

" It will become the best gard in the dis· trict ! "

" It will become the best gard in the dis- trict ! Do you think so ? Do you mean that ? "

" As surely as I am standing here ! "

" There, is not that just what I have said ? "

They both talked equally fast, and fitted together like the cogs of two wheels.

" But money, you see, money ? I have no money."

" We will get on slowly without money ; but get on we shall ! "

" Wo shall get on ! Of course we will.
But if wo *had* money, it would go faster you
say ? "

" Many times faster."

" Many times? We ought to have money !
Yes, yes; a man can chew who has not all his
teeth ; he who drives with oxen will get on,
too."

The mother stood blinking at Thore, who
gave her many quick side glances as he sat
swaying his body to and fro, and stroking his
knees with his hands. The school-master also
winked at him. Thore's lips parted, ho coughed
a little, and made an effort to speak ; but Ole
and Öyvind both kept on talking in an unin-
terrupted stream, laughed and kept up such a
clatter that no one else could be heard.

" You must be quiet for a little while, Thore
has something he wants to say," puts in the
school-master.

They pause and look at Thore, who finally
begins, in a low tone : —

" It has so happened that we have had a mill
on our place. Of late it has turned out that
we have had two. These mills have always
brought in a few shillings during the year; but
neither my father nor I have used any of these
shillings except while Öyvind was away. The

school-master has managed them, and he says they have prospered well where they are; but now it is best that Öyvind should take them for Nordistuen."

The mother stood in a corner, shrinking away into almost nothing, as she gazed with sparkling eyes at Thore, who looked very grave, and had an almost stupid expression on his face. Ole Nordistuen sat nearly opposite him, with wide-gaping mouth. Öyvind was the first to rouse from his astonishment, and burst out, —

" Does it not seem as if good luck went with me ! "

With this he crossed the floor to his father, and gave him a slap on the shoulder that rang through the room. " You, father ! " cried he, and rubbing his hands together he continued his walk.

" How much money might it be ? " finally asked Ole, in a low tone, of the school-master.

" It is not so little."

" Some hundreds? "

" Rather more."

" Rather more? Öyvind, rather more ! Lord help us, what a gard it will be ! "

He got up, laughing aloud.

" I must go with you up to Marit," says Öyvind. " We can use the conveyance that

is standing outside, then it will not take
long."

" Yes, at once! at once! Do *you*, too, want
everything done with haste ? "

" Yes, with haste and wrong."

" With haste and wrong! Just the way it
was with me when I was young, precisely."

" Here is your cap and staff; now I am going to drive you away."

" You are going to drive me away, ha—ha
—ha! But you are coming with me; are you
not? You are coming with me? All the rest
of you come along, too ; we must sit together
this evening as long as the coals are alive.
Come along!"

They promised that they would come. Öyvind helped Ole into the conveyance, and they
drove off to Nordistuen. The large dog was
not the only one up there who was surprised
when Ole Nordistuen came driving into the
gard with Öyvind Pladsen. While Öyvind was
helping Ole out of the conveyance, and servants and laborers were gaping at them, Marit
came out in the passage to see what the dog
kept barking at; but paused, as if suddenly
bewitched, turned fiery red, and ran in. Old
Ole, meanwhile, shouted so tremendously for
her when he got into the house that she had to
come forward again.

"Go and make yourself trim, girl; here is the one who is to have the gard!"

"Is that true?" she cries, involuntarily, and so loud that the words rang through the room.

"Yes; it is true!" replies Öyvind, clapping his hands.

At this she swings round on her toe, flings away what she has in her hand, and runs out; but Öyvind follows her.

Soon came the school-master, and Thore and his wife. The old man had ordered candles put on the table, which he had had spread with a white cloth. Wine and beer were offered, and Ole kept going round himself, lifting his feet even higher than usual; but the right foot always higher than the left.

Before this little tale ends, it may be told that five weeks later Öyvind and Marit were united in the parish church. The school-master himself led the singing on the occasion, for the assistant chorister was ill. His voice was broken now, for he was old; but it seemed to Öyvind that it did the heart good to hear him. When the young man had given Marit his hand, and was leading her to the altar, the school-master nodded at him from the chancel, just as Öyvind had seen him do, in fancy, when sitting sorrowfully at that dance long ago. Öyviud nodded back while tears welled up to his eyes.

These tears at the dance were the forerunners of those at the wedding. Between them lay Öyvind's faith and his work.

Here endeth the story of A HAPPY BOY.

LATER SKETCHES.

BLAKKEN.[1]

BJÖRGAN was in former times the parsonage of the parish of Kvikne, in the Dovrechain. It was situated far up the mountain, quite by itself. As a little boy, I often stood on the table in the family sitting-room, and gazing down into the valley, watched with wistful eyes those who in winter skimmed along the river on skates, or in summer sported on the green. Björgan lay so high that grain would not grow there, and therefore the gard was sold to a Swiss traveler, and a parsonage purchased in the valley, where the conditions are certainly somewhat better. The coming of winter at Björgan was sorrowfully early! A field, which father had sowed by way of experiment one warm, early spring, lay one morning covered with snow; the mown hay was in quite as great danger from a snow-storm as from a heavy fall of rain; and when winter overtook us the cold

---

[1] The name usually given to a dun-colored horse.

was so great that I dared not take hold of the
latch of the street door, lest my fingers should
freeze fast to the iron. My father, who was
born in that part of the country, near Rands-
fjord, and was thus well hardened to the cli-
mate, was, nevertheless, often compelled to
wear a mask over his face when he drove to
the distant sub-parish. The road creaked and
groaned when one person came walking along,
and beneath the footsteps of several it gave
forth a sharp, shrill sound. Snow often lay on
a level with the second story of the large building, while the smaller outhouses were entirely
buried in it; hills, shrubbery, and fences were
smoothed away, a sea of snow was spread around,
with the tops of the tall birch-trees floating on
its smooth surface, or it was lashed into billowy
undulations by a storm which had here made
hollows, there drifts. I stood on the table and
saw the swift runners on snow-shoes faring
away from us, down toward the valley. I saw
the Lapps come whizzing down the mountains
from the Röraas forest, with their reindeers,
and up the slope toward us. Their pulkhas
swayed to and fro, in the swift flight; and I
shall never forget the moment when the party
would finally draw up in our farm-yard, and a
ball of fur would creep out of each pulkha and

would prove to be a busy, cheery, little mortal, who sold reindeer meat.

The Kvikne dalesmen of latter days have developed into an enlightened, clever people; but at that time the Kvikne charge stood in worse repute than any other in the country. At not so very remote a date, a priest of that locality was obliged to carry pistols with him to church; another returned home from his church-ward trip and found all his furniture cut to pieces and destroyed, by men whose faces had been blackened, and who had almost frightened the life out of his wife, who was at home alone. The last priest had fled from the parish, and had positively refused to return. The charge had been without a pastor for many years, when father — perhaps just for that reason — was called to it, for he was considered capable of keeping a boat still against wind and storm.

I still remember distinctly how, one Saturday morning, I was in the act of creeping up-stairs to the study, on hands and feet, because there was a coating of ice on the steps after the scrubbing, and had not proceeded very far when a crash and din from the study drove me down again in terror. For one of the champions of the parish had undertaken up there to teach the refractory priest the ways of the people,

and had found to his dismay that the priest
was resolved to teach him first his own. He
made his exit from the door in such a manner
that he came tumbling all the way down to the
bottom of the stairs, and then gathering up his
limbs, he reached the street door in four bounds.
The people of Kvikne knew no better than to
suppose that the priest gave them the laws that
came from the Storthing. They wanted to forbid him to carry out the school laws; so, putting my father to defiance, they assembled in
great force at the meeting of the school board,
in order to hinder its actions with violence. In
spite of mother's earnest prayers, father had repaired thither, and as no one else had ventured
to aid him with the apportionment of the school
districts, etc., he did it himself, according to his
best judgment, amidst the thundering menaces
of the crowd; but when, with the register under his arm, he went out from the assembly,
they all gave way, and not a finger was laid on
him. My mother's rejoicing can readily be
imagined when she saw him driving home as
calm as ever.

Under such circumstances and surroundings
Blakken was born! His mother was a large
red mare from Gudbrandsdale, the delight of
every one who saw her; his sire was a madcap

of a black fjord horse, who, one fine day, in a
strange locality through which they were care-
lessly passing with the mare, burst whinnying
out of the forest, and bounding over fences and
ditches, came and took what was his own by
the right of love. Of Blakken it was early
said: "This will become the strongest horse
that has ever been seen here in the North;"
and accustomed as I was to stories about cham
pions and fights, I looked on the little foal as a
very highly-gifted comrade. He was, however,
not always good to me. I still bear a scar ove
the right eye, the work of his hoof; neverthe
less, I devoted myself with unwavering fidelity
to both mare and foal, slept with them in the
fields, and rolled between the mare's legs when
the foal was feeding. But once I went too
far with them. The day was warm; I had
fallen asleep inside of a woodland barn whose
door stood invitingly open, and where we had
doubtless all sought shade; the mare and the
foal had wandered farther, but I remained lying there. It was late in the day when those
who had been calling and searching for me in
vain came home with the tidings that I was
nowhere to be found. The reader can imagine
the alarm of my parents; every one joined in
the search, went shouting through field and

wood, carefully examined hills and precipices;
until at last a child was heard crying in a barn,
and I was found sitting on the hay. I was so
frightened that I could not speak; for a black
animal had been standing looking at me with
eyes of fire. Whether I had dreamed this or
actually experienced it, it would not be easy
to say; certain it is, though, that even a few
years ago I once awoke with this animal stand
ing over me.

Blakken and I soon had playfellows: first a
little dog that taught me to steal sugar, then
a cat that one day made its appearance in the
kitchen. I had never seen a cat before, and,
pale as a corpse, I rushed into the sitting-room,
screaming that a large mouse had come up
from the cellar! The next spring our numbers were still further increased by the addition of a little pig; and then as often as Blakken accompanied his mother when she went
about her work, the dog, the cat, the pig, and I
came trooping after. We managed to kill time
pretty successfully, especially by taking naps
together. Indeed, I shared with these playfellows everything I liked myself: thus I once
carried a silver spoon out to the pig, in order
that it might eat nicer; and it tried, too, that
is to say, to eat the silver spoon. When I

accompanied my parents down to the valley to
see people, the dog, the cat, and the pig went
along. The first two were taken into the
ferry-boat that was to carry us across the river,
the pig, with a little grunt, then swam after us.
We were treated to refreshments, each to suit
his taste, and in the evening we went home
again in the same manner.

But soon it was my fate to lose these comrades and retain only Blakken; for my father
was called to the parish Næsset in Romsdal.
It was a memorable day when we set forth, we
children and a nurse-maid stowed away in a
little house, secured firmly on a long sledge,
that neither wind nor snow might assail us,
and my father and mother in a double sleigh
in front of us, surrounded by a group of people
who wanted to say farewell over and over
again. I cannot say that I was especially sorrowful; for I was only six years old, and I
knew that at Trondhjem there was to be
bought for me a hat and coat and trousers
that I was to put on when we got to our journey's end! And there, in our new home, I
was to see the sea for the first time! And
then, too, Blakken was with us.

Here at the Næsset parsonage, one of the fin
est gards in the country, lying broad-breasted

between two arms of the fjord, with green
mountains above and cataracts and gards on
the opposite shore, with undulating fields and
eager life in the heart of the valley, and out
along the fjord mountains, from which naze
after naze, with a large gard on each, project
out into the water, — here at the Næsset parsonage, where I could stand of evenings and
watch the play of the sun over mountain and
fjord until I wept as if I had done something
wrong; and where on my snow-shoes, down
in some valley or other, I could suddenly
pause, as one spell-bound by a beauty, a yearning, which I was powerless to explain, but
which was so great that I felt the most exalted
joy as well as the most oppressive sense of im-
prisonment and grief; here at the Næsset parsonage my impressions grew, and one of the
liveliest of these was that made on me by Blakken; for here he, also, grew. He became a
hero, and did heroic work.

He was not very tall, but was extremely long
in proportion to his height, and of a breadth
that called forth an involuntary smile in the
beholder; he was of a dun hue, rather inclined
to the yellow than the white, with a black,
extraordinarily full mane , he became a heavy
good-natured beast — in his every-day work, al

ways hanging his head. His accustomed duties he performed as calmly as an ox, but most effectually. In addition to accomplishing more than half the horse-labor of the farming, wood-hauling, etc., on this very inconvenient gard, he did more than half the labor of hauling materials for a large, new main house and for the many additional buildings my father erected besides, and hauled it from a far-distant, awful forest. Where two horses could not pull the load, Blakken was used, and if the harness held he would bring it through. He liked to look over his shoulder at the boys while they piled on his double and triple load; of course he had not much to say about it, but he had to be told to go three or four times before he would heed the order, and even, then, he always first made a few trial pulls, — and then he started. He took his time, step by step. Sometimes there came a new servant who wanted to practice him in a swifter pace, but it always ended by the boy's learning the horse's gait. The lash was never used; for the powerful laborer soon became so dearly beloved that he was managed entirely by caresses. As Blakken gradually became renowned in the parishes, it came to be an honor, indeed, to drive him.

For Blakken was soon beyond compare the

greatest wonder of the diocese. It began, as
is always the case when anything great starts
up, with terrible uproar and hatred; it began,
namely, by Blakken, who went out in the forest
and on the mountain among the other horses of
the parish, insisting on claiming all the mares
for himself. He so severely bruised and gashed
his rival suitors, who fancied that they could
compete with him, that the peasants came rushing down to the parsonage with solemn im-
precations and demands for damages. They
thought it best, however, to have patience,
when they saw that they would be indemnified
under all circumstances; for Blakken's off-
spring did him honor! Still, it was for a long
time a source of annoyance that his superiority
was so immense and indisputable. Our neighbor, the lieutenant, could not, as a soldier, sub-
mit to this; he secured two heavily-built Gud-
brands-dale horses, splendid animals, — and
they were to teach Blakken respect. There
were many wagers laid for and against; and
how excited we were about the issue of the
first encounter in the spring, up in the mount-
ain-pasture! I shall, therefore, never forget the
beautiful Whitsun evening when, as I stood
out of doors listening to the black-grouse that
were frolicking on the slope, a girl came run-

ning up and announced that both of the lieutenant's horses were standing close by the
grindstone, near at hand, pressed up against
each other. All hastened to the spot; and
lo! the two superb animals stood trembling
there, with blood streaming from wound after
wound, — they had been under Blakken's mon-
strous hoofs and teeth! Terror had endowed
them with strength to leap over the high picket
fence of the parsonage; for they had not dared
to pause before they had reached the house.
The next day Blakken's praise was sounded
along the church wall and was borne from
there over mountain and strand.

Blakken had the sorrow of having one of his
own sons, a spirited brown horse, share his
sway with him for some years. He caught
him in the midst of his first revolt, and as this
audacious son would not take flight, but sent
forth a challenging war-cry, the tried champion
raised himself; they approached each other on
their hind legs, threw their fore legs round
each other's necks and wrestled. (Stallions
always fight in this way.) Soon the young
madcap described the arc of a violin bow;
shortly after he lay crushed on the ground,
and received his paternal chastisement. This
I myself witnessed.

Almost every summer there were bears in the
woods that killed many cows and sheep both
for us and others. We were constantly startled
by hearing the herd-boys halloo and the shep-
herd dogs bay; then the bells would ring, and
the working people hasten to assemble and
start for the woods with guns, axes, and iron
bars; but as a rule their coming would be too
late: either the dog would already have driven
away the bear, or else the cattle had been
stricken down ere help arrived. The horses
could better defend themselves; but it happened now and then that the bear killed a
horse, either by luring him into a swamp, where
the horse sank and became an easy victim, or
by getting him started on a race, so that he
would plunge over a cliff.

One summer things were especially bad;
there was scarcely a week that the bear did not
attack our cattle; the horses would suddenly
make their appearance close by the cattle pen,
in a state of frantic alarm; for every time they
had been chased by the bear. But Blakken,
with the mare and the foal, which he with his
sharp shoes held guard over, never came. We
were in despair at last to know what had happened to them; the herd-boys had not heard
the mare's bell for many days. As there had

been a long-continued storm, during which the horses are apt to seek shelter near home, indeed often to station themselves just outside of the inclosure leading to the stable, and still they had not come, the boys were sent up into the woods in strong force in quest of them. They searched chiefly about the marshy lands, to see whether the bear might not have enticed thither the combat-loving horse, and thus overcome him and afterwards perhaps have taken both the foal and the mare, which naturally would have defended the foal. They sought and sought without detecting anything suspicious; the bear's footsteps (tracks as they are called) were everywhere to be seen, but no sign of any fight with a horse. As the boys walked on talking of this, and approached one of the finest grazing-grounds in the whole forest, one of them observed that just in the vicinity of a swamp there were tracks of the foal and the mare, but that they had been going round and round without stopping in the same circle, consequently in great alarm, and that this had happened recently, probably that same day. Upon examining the marsh they found truly enough that it had been torn up by the feet in a great fight. The boys began to feel hot and cold in turn, but they were determined to examine into

the matter more thoroughly. On the brink of
the swamp they saw traces of the hind feed
both of bear and horse; they must then have
both drawn themselves up at once, while the
bear walked backward out in the swamp, in
order to mislead the horse, and the latter followed; for the swamp can easily uphold the
broad paw and calf of the bear; because he is
not as heavy as the horse, who quickly sinks in
and is caught there. But this time the bear
had miscalculated; for although Blakken had
sunk in pretty badly, the gigantic strength of
his loins had sufficed to raise his legs from the
mire of the swamp, while the sharp-shod fore-
feet beat, and the sharp teeth tore, and soon
there could be found no further traces of the
bear's hind-feet, but, on the other hand, an exact
impression of his furry hide, and this was repeated over and over again through the whole
swamp. He had been thrown down, had not
been able to pick himself up again, but had
turned over, and rolled round and round, in order to protect himself from the blows and bites
of the infuriated horse, and this could be traced
all the way to firm land. Inflamed by the ex-
citing story of the battle-field, the hearing of
the boys became sharpened, their sight more
keen, and now in the still atmosphere, all glit

tering with sunbeams after the rainy weather, they could hear the mare's bell from the leafy wood at the foot of the ridge. They hastened thither, but were met by Blakken who with flashing eyes forbade them to come nearer. He was scarcely to be recognized. With head thrown back and floating mane, he was trotting round the mare and the foal in a large circle, and it was only after much kind talk and with the aid of salt, which they carried with them, that they could get him to recognize that these were friends who had come.

Now this, Blakken's great achievement, which was unique of its kind, threw such a halo about the animal's name that from being known as "the priest's Blakken," he was promoted to the title "Bear Blakken." Time upon time, year after year, he had his wrestles with the bear, and each time was long uncontrollable. He once came home bearing marks of the bear's claws; the fight had been with an old warrior who had seized the horse below the eyes, and had made terrible gashes there when Blakken had torn his head loose. To have such a fierce old stallion going sharp-shod about the woods and pastures was extremely dangerous; but the horses knew him and fled at his approach, and even if now and then one would be stupid

enough to allow himself to get a thrashing,
people were inclined to be forbearing with
Blakken, on account of his great fame.   A
horse who could throw the bear to the ground
might be allowed to do pretty much as he
pleased.

How greatly admired he was could best be
seen when we were obliged, as seldom happened, to employ him as a church horse.   If
the whole family with the governess and tutor
wanted to drive to church, he had to draw three
or four of us in an old gig, in which one sat
"not merely for pleasure."   As none of the
ordinary harnesses were large enough for him,
he had to hobble along in his working gear, and
as his heavy bristling mane fell over his eyes,
he did not look exactly suitable for a trip to
church.   He had to be put in the rear of the
party; for in the first place he would not trot,
but would only take the gait suitable for a
working cart, and, in the second place, he
wanted to carry the church-going people into
all the woodland paths he was accustomed to
tread.   But if he went in the rear, he did to
a certain extent as the others did; when the
other horses trotted, Blakken plunged forward,
and so those who sat in the gig were borne
onward at a hobbling jerking pace, or as in a

heavy sea, and on one occasion were actually made sea-sick. At church, on the other hand, there was an entire change. There were a great many other horses there, and throwing back his head he would send forth a veritable war-whoop. It would be answered from the fields round about, and off he would start with the gig, but would be held back, unharnessed, and tethered. He had his own special tether along, and was always tied in a place close to the foot of the mountain, in order to be as far as possible from the other horses. But if he wanted to join them, he would tug at his tether and raise himself on his hind legs, and send a long whinny down the slope. A larger number of people gathered about him than were seated in church; when he had been quiet a while, they would pat him, measure his breast, his neck, his hips, would take him by the mouth, in order to examine his jaws; but as soon as one of the other horses neighed, he would tear himself away from his admirers, start up and reply; this seemed to all beholders the noblest sight they had ever seen. I for my part have certainly never since been so proud of anything as I was in those days of Blakken, when I stood among the peasants, and listened to their loud resounding words of praise.

And here, at the summit of his triumphal career, let me leave him. I went forth into the world and found other goals for my admiration and other heroes to follow.

FIDELITY.

Yonder on the plains in my native parish, there dwelt a husband and wife with their six sons. They toiled faithfully on a very large but hitherto neglected gard, until an accidental wound from an axe ended the husband's days, and the wife was left alone with the hard work and the six children. She did not lose her courage, but led her eldest two sons forward to the side of the coffin, and made them promise her over their father's corpse to care for their little brothers and sisters, and to be a help to her as far as God gave them strength. They promised, and they kept their word until the youngest son was confirmed. Then they considered themselves released from their pledge; the eldest married the widow of a gardman, and the next to the eldest shortly afterward married her well-to-do sister.

The four brothers who remained at home were to have the entire management, after

having until now been continually under control themselves. They did not feel much ambition for this; from childhood up they had
been accustomed to keep together, either in
couples or all four, and did so more than ever
now that they must depend solely on one another for help. Not one of them would state
his own opinion about anything until he felt
sure of that of the others; indeed they were
not certain of their own opinions until they
had looked into one another's faces. Without
having made any compact, there was still a
mute agreement among them, that they would
never separate as long as their mother lived.

She herself, however, preferred to have
things somewhat differently arranged, and got
the two who had already left home to agree
with her. The gard had become a well-tilled
piece of land; more help was needed, and so
the mother proposed to pay the eldest two for
their portion, and divide the gard among the
four sons at home, in such a way that they
would keep together in couples, each couple
occupying half of the gard. There should be
erected a new set of houses alongside of the old
ones; two of the sons should take possession of
them; the other two should remain with her.
But of the couple that left home, one must

marry; for they would need help about the
house and the cattle; and the mother named
the girl whom she would like to have for a
daughter-in-law.

None of them had any objections to offer,
but now the question arose, which two should
move away, and of these two, which one should
marry? The eldest of the four said that he
was quite willing to leave home, but he would
never marry; and each of the others in turn
objected.

Finally they agreed with the mother that
the girl should be allowed to decide the matter. And up at the summer stable one evening
the mother asked her if she would be willing
to come to the plains as a wife, and the girl
proved to be quite willing. Well, then, which
of the boys would she like to marry; for she
could have whichever one she pleased. Why,
she had not considered the matter. Then she
must do so now, for it was left to her to decide. Well, then, she supposed it might be the
eldest; but him, she was told, she could not
have; he was not willing. Then the girl
named the youngest. But the mother thought
there would oe something strange in that :
" for he was the youngest."

" Then the next to the youngest!"

" Why not the next to the eldest ? "

" To be sure, why not the next to the eldest ? " replied the girl ; for he was the one she
had been thinking of the whole time, therefore
had not dared name him.

Now the mother had judged, from the moment the eldest had refused, that this must be
because he thought the next to the eldest and
the girl had an eye on each other. So the
next to the eldest married the girl, and the
eldest moved with him into the new home.
How the gard was now divided no outsider
could learn, for the brothers worked together
as they had done before, and they stored away
their harvest, now in one barn, now in the
other.

After a time the mother's health began to
fail; she needed rest, consequently, help, and
the sons agreed to engage permanently a girl
who was in the habit of working here. The
youngest brother was to ask the girl the next
day they were gathering leaves ; he knew her
best. Now the youngest must for some time
have had a secret liking for this girl; for when
he came to speak to her he did it in such a singular manner that she thought he was asking
her to marry him, and she said, " Yes." The
youth was frightened, and going at once to his

brothers told them what a mistake had been made. They all four became very grave, and none of them dared utter the first word. But the next to the youngest could see that the youngest really cared for the girl, and that was the reason why he was so frightened. At the same time he saw clearly that it was his own lot to be a bachelor; for if the youngest should marry he could not. This seemed to him rather hard, for there was one of whom he himself had thought; but now nothing could come of that. It was *he*, then, who made the first remark, namely, that they would be surest of the girl if she should come to the gard as the wife of one of them. Always when one had spoken the others agreed, and the brothers now went to talk with their mother. But when they got home they found their mother ill in earnest; they must wait until she was well; and as she did not become well again, they once more held counsel together. In it the youngest proposed that as long as the mother lay in bed no change must be made, and this was agreed to; for the girl must have no more to care for than the mother. Thus it remained.

For sixteen years the mother lay in bed. For sixteen years the intended daughter-in-law

waited on her patiently and without a murmur.
For sixteen years the sons met every evening
for devotions at her bedside, and on Sundays
the eldest two also joined them. She often
begged them in these peaceful hours to remember her who had tended her; they understood
what she meant by this, and promised. During all these sixteen years she blessed her ill-
ness, because it had allowed her to taste a
mother's joy to the last; she thanked them
every time they gathered about her bedside, —
and one day this was for the last time.

When she was dead her six sons met to bear
her themselves to the grave. It was customary
here for women as well as men to attend funer-
als, and this time the whole parish followed,
men and women, all who were able to walk,
even the children; — first the deacon, as leader
of the singing, then the six sons with the coffin, and then a long train of people, all singing so that they were heard more than a mile
away. And when the body was laid to rest,
and the six sons had filled the grave, the
whole procession repaired to the church, for
there the youngest son was to be married; the
brothers would have it so, because this funeral
and wedding really belonged together. Here
the priest, who was my now deceased father,
spoke so eloquently of fidelity that I, who

chanced to be present, thought when I came out of church that it was something that belonged with the mountains and the sea and the grandeur of the entire surrounding nature.

———◆———

" WHY shall we sit down here ? "

" Because it is high and light."

" But there is an awful precipice here; it makes me giddy, and the sun glares on the water. Let us go farther! "

" No; no farther."

" Then let us go back to the green glen; it was so beautiful there."

" Oh, no; not there either," and he sank down as though he could not or would not keep up longer.

She remained standing, with her eyes fixed intently on him.

Finally he said, " Aasta, you must now explain to me why you were so afraid of the foreign skipper who came in at twilight."

" Was not that what I thought," she whispered, and acted as though she wanted to run away.

" You must tell me this before you go, else I will not follow you."

" Botolf!" she exclaimed, and turned round, but did not stir from the spot.

"It is true, I have promised you not to ask," said he. " I will keep my word, too, if you prefer to have it so ; but in that case it is all over between us."

Now she burst into tears, and walked right up in front of him. Her delicate little figure, her soft, light hair, from which the kerchief had fallen back, and then her eyes and mouth, — each strikingly individual and yet combined now in one expression ; the sun was shining full upon her. He sprang to his feet.

" Ah, you know very well when you look thus at me, I always yield. But I have now also learned that it is only worse afterward. Cannot you understand this : if I promise you a hundred times not to want to know your past, I can have no peace. I cannot endure it ! "

His face, too, bore traces of a suffering that did not date from yesterday.

" Bo. lf, that was just what you promised me, at th time when you would never let me have peace, you promised me to let it all rest, all that I could never, never tell you. You promised me this solemnly ; you said that it made no difference to you ; that it was only

me you wanted! Botolf!"—and she sank
down on her knees in the heather in front of
him; she wept as though her life were in peril;
she gazed at him, while tear after tear continued to speak for her, and she was the most
beautiful and most unhappy being he had ever
in his life beheld.

"God have mercy on me," said he, as he
rose, but sat down again at once; "if you
loved me enough to place confidence in me,
how happy we two might be together!"

"And if you could only have a little confidence in me," she besought, drawing nearer to
him on her knees, and then she continued:
"Love you? That night when I came up on
deck, after our ship had run against yours, you
stood by the shrouds, giving orders. I had
never seen anything so strong. I loved you at
once! And when you carried me over into the
boat while the ship was sinking, I felt a desire
for life again, and that I had thought I never
more should feel."

She ceased speaking, and she wept; but
presently she clasped her hands on his knee.
"Botolf!" she implored, "be great; be mag-
nanimous, as you were that time when you
took me, without anything else,—only me!—
Botolf!"

Almost harshly, he replied, "Why do you tempt me? You know very well I cannot! It is the soul we want; it is not this. In the first days it is all very well, but not afterwards!"

She drew back, and said, hopelessly, "Oh, no! A life can never become whole again. Oh, my God!" Then she burst into tears.

"Give me your whole life, and not merely a fragment of it! and then it shall become whole again in my keeping!" He spoke with emphasis, as though to put courage into her; she made no reply, but he saw that she was undergoing a struggle. "Conquer yourself! Have courage! Worse than it is now, it cannot possibly be!"

"You can drive me to the worst!" she wailed. He misunderstood her, and continued: "Even if it proved to be the greatest crime, I shall try to bear it; but this I cannot bear."

"No, nor I either!" she cried, and rose.

"I will help you!" he rose too, as he spoke; "every single day I will help you, if I but know what it is. But I am too proud to be the keeper of something I do not know—and which may perhaps belong to another!"

Here she grew flaming red. "For shame!" she cried. "Of us two, I am the prouder. I do

not offer what belongs to another   Now you
may cease!"

"Ah, if you are proud, take away my suspicion!"

"Good Lord, I can endure this no longer!"

"No, I have sworn that *this day* shall bring
the *end!*"

"Is it not merciless," she cried, "to be willing to torment and torture a woman who has
trusted herself to you, and who has prayed to
be spared, as fervently as I have!" and her
tears began to flow again, but with a sudden
revulsion of feeling she burst out: "I understand you; you want to force that which is
within me to cry aloud, so that you may thus
learn something."

She looked at him resentfully and turned
away.   Then she heard slowly, word for word:

"Will you, or will you not?"

She stretched forth her hand.   "Not if you
were to offer me all that now lies spread before
our eyes!"

She walked from him, her bosom heaving,
her eyes restlessly wandering about, but chiefly
seeking his face with an expression that was
now hard, now agonized, now hard again.   She
leaned against a tree and wept, then she ceased
weeping, but walked on as before.

" I knew very well that you did not love me," she heard, and in a moment was the humblest and most repentant of women.

She made several efforts to reply, but instead flung herself down on the heather and buried her face in her hands. He walked up to her and stood over her. She felt him standing there, she waited for him to speak, she covered her face, but as no words came, she grew still more frightened and had to look up. As she did so she sprang to her feet; his weather-beaten long face had become hollow, his deep eyes that were without eyebrows, his wide mouth, with its tightly compressed lips, his whole large, imposing figure, became impressed with such a concentrated, extraordinary force upon her that she suddenly saw him standing up by the shrouds, as on the night of the shipwreck. He had become as grand as he was then, and possessed of a boundless strength, but this strength was now turned against herself!

" You have lied to me, Aasta!" She retreated, but he came after her. " You have also made a liar of me; *there has not been perfect truth between us one single day of the time we have lived together!*"

He stood so near her that she could feel his warm breath; he looked right into her eyes until she grew dizzy; she did not know what she should say or do the next moment, and so she closed her eyes. She stood as though either about to fall down or to run away — the crisis was at hand. In the profound silence that preceded it, he himself grew alarmed. Once more he assailed her: —

"Give me proof! Lay aside all your arts; do it now, here!"

"Yes!" replied she, but without being conscious that she spoke.

"Do it now, here!" I say.

He gave a shriek; for at this moment, she dashed past him and over the brink of the steep; he saw her fair hair, her upward stretched hands, a kerchief that floated up, got loose, and fluttering after her was soon wafted far away. He heard no scream, nor a yet splash, for the depth was very great. Nor did he *listen;* for he had fallen to the ground.

From the sea she had come to him that night, in the sea she had disappeared, and with her the history of her life. Into the black night of the deep had plunged all that his soul possessed — should he not follow? He had come hither with the firm determination to put an end to his torment; this was no end, the end could now never come, this was only the real

beginning. Her last act shouted up to him that
he had judged falsely and murdered her! Notwithstanding this the agony had increased ten-
fold; he must live in order to ponder on how it
had come to pass. She, who was almost the
only one who was saved that terrible night, she
had been rescued only to be murdered by him
who had rescued her. He who had sailed about
and traded as though the whole world was only
a sea and a place of business, had suddenly become the victim of a love which had destroyed
both him and the object of his affections. Was
he wicked? He had never heard this said, and
never felt it. But what was it, then? He
rose — not to fling himself over the precipice,
but to go down the mountain again; he would
not put an end to his life the moment he had
found a problem to solve.

But it could never be solved. She had lived
in America ever since she was grown up; she
was coming from there when the ship struck.
Where in America should he begin? Where
she was from in Norway he did not definitely
know; he was not even sure that her surname
was the one her family had borne in Norway.
The foreign skipper? Ah, where was he?
And did he know her, or was it only she who
knew him? He might as well ask the sea; to

journey away and begin an investigation was the same thing as to plunge into it.

He had been in error! One who was guilty and repentant would have eased her mind by confessing all to her husband; one who was not repentant would have sought to evade his inquiries. But she revealed nothing, nor did she seek evasion; she took refuge in death when pressed too sorely. Such courage did not belong to one who was guilty. Ah, why not? Rather death than confession; for still greater courage was needed for the latter. But she did not lack the nerve for confession; for she had certainly begun by confessing that there was something she could not tell him. It must be a crime that forbade it. But she could not have been guilty of any great crime; for she had often been happy, indeed merry; she was passionate, but she had fine feelings and was kind-hearted. The crime must be that of another. Why, then, not say that it was that of another; for in such a case his distrust would have vanished. But if it were neither hers nor that of another, what was it, then? She herself had certainly said that there was something — and then the foreign skipper of whom she was so much afraid? What was it, what in the name of wonder could it be? Had she still lived, he

would still have continued to torment her —
this thought stung him and made him wretched.

And his agonies did not cease. Perhaps she
was not so guilty as she thought herself, or perhaps not so guilty as she must seem to others.
How often is there not innocence behind our
guilt, simplicity in sin, although so few can understand it — and *him* she had not believed
capable of understanding it, because he was
in a continual state of suspicion. Out of one
straightforward answer he would have found
occasion for a thousand suspicious questions, and
therefore she had preferred to trust herself to
death than to him! Why, had he never, never
been able to leave her in peace? To *him* she
had fled from her past, of *him* she had sought
protection from it, and yet it was he who was
constantly conjuring it up, and who continually
let it loose upon her! She was truly devoted
to him, she was affectionate and charming when
with him — what then was her past to him?
And if it did concern him, why had he not
thought of it at first? No, according as her
tenderness increased, his restlessness grew; the
moment she became his, not only from admiration and gratitude, but from the heart, then he
wanted to know if she had ever belonged to any
one else, and what her previous life had been.

And the more it grieved her, the more she begged for mercy, the more he insisted, for he felt sure there must be something!

For the first time the thought occurred to him: had *he* told *her* everything? Was it really imperative to tell each other everything? Would all be understood as it really was? Most assuredly not.

He heard two children playing near him, and looked round. He sat in the green glen she had recently spoken of, but he was not aware of it until now. Five hours had rolled by, he thought it was but a few minutes. The children must have been playing here for some time, but he had not heard them until now. Ah! was not that Agnes, the priest's six or eight years old daughter? whom Aasta had loved to idolatry, and who was so much like her — God in Heaven; how like her she was! The child had just helped her little brother up on a stone, he was to play being in school, and she was to be the school-master.

"Now say what I say," said she. "Our Father!"

"Ou' Fath'!"

"Who art in heaven!"

"Heaven!"

"Hallowed be thy name."

" Ha'o'ed ey name."

" Thy kingdom come."

" No!"

" Thy will be done."

" No, I will not."

Botolf had stolen away walking backward; it was not the prayer which affected him, he had not even perceived at first that it was a prayer, but while he listened to and watched the children he suddenly appeared in his own eyes like a foul beast of prey, thrust out from fellowship with God and with man. Behind the bushes he retreated, that the children might not discover his presence; he was more afraid of them than he had ever been of anything in his whole life. He stole into the forest, far from the highway. Whither should he go? To the empty house he had bought and made ready for her? Or farther away? It mattered not; for wherever he could imagine himself, there she stood before him.

It is said of dying people that they have mirrored in their eyes the last thing they have seen, and he who awakens from an evil deed carries with him the first object his eyes rest on and never more becomes free from it. It was not Aasta he saw, as he had seen her lately on the heights; it was a little innocent girl—it was

Agnes. Even the image of Aasta as she sank from his sight became transformed into that of the child, with its small, uplifted hands. The remembrance of Aasta's unspeakable love for the child caused the images within his soul to undergo a mysterious change, the strong likeness played into the doubt of long months as to whether Aasta was guilty or innocent. Had Aasta just such a child nature concealed within her own breast? Yes, he had seen this, or rather, he knew now for the first time that he had seen it. Until now he had merely brooded over whether hers was the expression of innocence, whether she could have smiled thus to more than one, or in what way it was she had veiled this child she bore within her heart since it only had power to burst forth in radiant moments. A continual variableness in her nature, a restlessness with perpetual exaggeration, which also led others to exaggeration, had in her life both attracted and repelled him; now after her sorrowful death, all remembrances were centred in an innocent child engaged in prayer.

Where thought was piteously searching for light, he met the child; this barred every avenue to investigation. Every scene in their short life together, from that night of ship-

wreck until the Sunday morning on the heights
— whenever he would question it, the child's
face appeared, and this singular confusion of
the two so wearied him in body and mind that
after the lapse of a few days he was scarcely
able to take any food, and ere long he was un-
able to leave his bed.

Every one saw that this was tending toward
death. He who himself is the bearer of a problem, acquires a peculiar presence which makes
him a problem to others. From the day he
took possession here, *his* gloomy silence, *her*
beauty and the hidden life of both created much
gossip in the parish; when the wife suddenly
disappeared the excitement grew until the most
incredible things were the most readily believed.
No one could furnish any information, inasmuch
as none of those who lived or were occupied
along the sea-shore or the mountain ridges, had
had a view of the heights that Sunday morning
just at the moment when she had flung herself
over the precipice in the sunshine. Nor did her
body drift ashore to bear witness itself. There
were therefore stories afloat about him, even
during his lifetime. He presented an ugly appearance, as he lay there in his bed, with his
long, hollow face, which was surrounded by an
unbroken framework of red beard and bristling

red hair. The large eyes looked up as from a shut-in lake. As he seemed neither to want to live nor to die, it was said that there was a struggle about him between God and the devil. Some had even seen the evil one, surrounded by flames of fire, reach up to the windows of his chamber in order to call him. They had seen him sniffing around the house in the form of a black dog, or bounding in front of it like a rolling ball of wool. People who were rowing past had seen the whole gard on fire, others had heard a procession shouting, barking, laughing aloud, coming out of the sea, faring slowly toward the house, passing in through closed doors, rushing madly through all the rooms, and then with the same screaming, baying of dogs and neighing of horses, sweeping down to the sea again and there disappearing.

The servants of the sick man, men and women, left at once, and they told about all these things. No one dared go near the gard. Had not an old houseman and his wife, to whom he had been kind, now taken pity on him, he would have been left without any help. The old woman who waited on him was herself in great fear: she burned straw under his bed, in order to drive away the evil one; but although the sick man was nearly destroyed by fire, released he was not. He lay there in terrible suffering. The old woman thought finally that there must be some one for whom he was waiting. She asked him if a message should be sent for the priest. He shook his head. Was there any one else he would like to see? To this he made no reply. The next day, as he lay on his bed, he distinctly pronounced the name "Agnes." It surely did not come as an answer to her question of the preceding day; but the old woman took it for this. Delighted, she got up from her seat, and going out to her husband begged him make haste to harness the horse and drive over to the priest's for Agnes.

At the parsonage they thought there was surely a mistake, and that it was the priest who was wanted to minister to the sick; but the old man insisted upon it that it was Agnes. The little girl herself sat within listening, and was much afraid; for she also had heard about the devil and the procession from the sea; but she had also heard that the sick man was waiting to see some one before he could die, and did not think it was strange that it should be her whom his wife had so often carried home with her. The wishes of a dying person must be fulfilled, they told Agnes, and if she prayed like a good girl to her God, then no one could do her any harm. And she believed this, and permitted herself to be dressed for the visit.

It was a cold clear evening, with long attendant shadows, the sleigh-bells were echoed through the woods, it was somewhat alarming; but Agnes sat in the sleigh and prayed, her hands clasped inside of her muff. She did not see the devil, nor did she hear the procession from the sea, along whose strand she was driving; but she saw the stars above her, and the light on the heights in front of her. Up at the gard it was dismally still; but the old woman came out at once, carried her in, took off her travelling wraps, and bade her warm herself at the stove. And, meanwhile, the old woman said that she must be of good cheer and go bravely forward to the sick man and say the Lord's Prayer over him. When she was warm, the old woman took her by the hand and led her into the chamber. There he lay, with his long beard and his large and hollow eyes, staring at her. She did not think that he was ugly, and she was not afraid.

"Will you forgive me?" he whispered.

She knew that she ought to say Yes, and so she said Yes. Then he smiled and tried to raise himself, but was powerless to do so. She began at once with the Lord's Prayer, but he made a movement of protest, and pointed to his breast; and now she laid her two hands on it, for that was what she understood him to mean, and he laid his clammy, ice-cold, bony hand above her little warm hands and then closed his eyes. As he said nothing when she had finished, she did not venture to withdraw her hands, but began anew. When she had done this for the third time the old woman came in, looked at them and said, —

"You may stop, my child, for now he is released."